The Peanut Butter Poltergeist

Also by Ellen Leroe

Confessions of a Teenage TV Addict
Have a Heart, Cupid Delaney
The Plot Against the Pom-Pom Queen
Robot Romance

Ellen Leroe

The Peanut Butter Poltergeist

illustrated by Jacqueline Rogers

Lodestar Books · E. P. Dutton · New York

No character in this book is intended to represent any actual person; all the incidents of the story are entirely fictional in nature.

Library of Congress Cataloging in Publication Data

Leroe, Ellen.
    The Peanut Butter Poltergeist.

    "Lodestar books."
    Summary: Eleven-year-old M.J. seeks revenge on his obnoxious stepsister by faking evidence of a poltergeist in their summer cottage, only to face the horror of what seems to be a real poltergeist.
    [1. Poltergeists—Fiction. 2. Stepchildren—Fiction]
I. Rogers, Jackie, ill. II. Title.
PZ7.L5614Pe 1987 [Fic] 87-8882
ISBN 0-525-67241-9

Published in the United States by E. P. Dutton, 2 Park Avenue, New York, N.Y. 10016, a division of NAL Penguin Inc.

Published simultaneously in Canada by Fitzhenry & Whiteside Limited, Toronto

Editor: Rosemary Brosnan   Designer: Alice Lee Groton

Printed in the U.S.A.   W   First Edition
10 9 8 7 6 5 4 3 2 1

For Jane Mary Leroe,
one of the original Peanut Butter Kids.
And for her family:
Peter S., Peter B., Thomas, and Mary.

1

Call me Michael J. Garrett.

Or call me Chicken Little.

But whatever you do, don't call me the Peanut Butter Poltergeist. I got into enough trouble this past summer over this scary creature.

You'd think I would have known better than to get involved in a silly kid's game with my new stepsister. I'm eleven, for pete's sake, and a down-to-earth kid. My stepsister, Ashley, the former Python Princess, never blinked at ghost stories or horror movies, either.

But for two weeks this past June, we both didn't quite know what to believe. Until we found out the truth . . .

It all happened in a spooky old house my family rented near Black Lake, in Pennsylvania. We learned from the real estate agent that it was supposed to be haunted. I laughed—but then I got an idea. M.J. Garrett's big brainstorm. It was all intended to be a joke, but it turned into something else.

Something to do with things that go thump in the night, a possessed jar of peanut butter, and a scene that happened at Black Lake just like in a Stephen King novel.

It was out near the woods, by Black Lake.

It happened at midnight and the night was rainy and thundery . . . and creepy.

I saw something move in the shadows.

I felt something icicle-cold dance down my spine, and that's when I realized the game wasn't a game anymore.

But wait! Let me start at the very beginning. Saturday, June 20, to be exact, was the date the whole adventure with our peanut butter poltergeist began.

I wish I could begin with "It was a dark and stormy night," but I can't. If I remember right, it was a beautiful, warm sunny day.

The Garrett family took their first official vacation together the third week of June, after school was out. Since my dad had married Cora Lynn, or Cory as she wanted me to call her, only a week before, I hadn't had much time to get to know her daughter, Ashley.

Ash was tall, lanky, and twelve—going on obnoxious. She had long dirty-blonde hair that hid most of her face, *Children of the Damned* eyes that could look straight through you and not register a thing, and a stuffed animal collection that made a toy store's look positively shabby.

I went to Garfield School in Philadelphia, but she went to some snobby girls' school where she learned how to play the flute, to ride horses, and to win athletic letters in the strangest sports imaginable: lacrosse, badminton, archery. She was a know-it-all and a royal pain and there was no way, no way at all, that we would ever be friends.

Friends. Ha! That was like asking a Mets fan and a Dodgers fan to sit down and shake hands. No chance was this two-week vacation going to work. For one thing, the small town of Langtown, PA, was *my* town. My dad and I had been coming here every summer since my mom died six years ago. I knew practically everyone in Langtown. With a population of only 65, that wasn't too difficult. And I had special friends here, too—David and Berry DeRemer. I had memories of private times shared with my father and private places only we knew about. And I didn't want Ash horning in on my territory.

Or in on my father, either.

He had already bought her a stuffed panda, which had made her squeal, and now she was asking him to help carry her dumb flute case and the box of cutesy teddy bears, pandas, and polar bears. We had just pulled up to the summer rental house, way off R.D. 2, on River Road, and Cory stuck her head out the window. She examined the rather dilapidated monstrosity for what seemed like a long time, while my father whistled nervously beside her.

Then she turned back to face us with a bright smile on her face, the kind Mrs. DeMaio wears when our principal pays her a surprise visit.

"It's very—uh—picturesque, Mark," she said to my father. "I'm sure it'll be fine for two weeks."

She hated it, too, I thought. I'm not the only one. My father gave a short nod, and got out of the car. I jumped out my side and Ash and Cory got out. As if examining a modernistic painting we didn't understand or appreciate, the four of us stood there silently and examined the house. It's so ugly, it's almost funny, I thought. It might even be fun to spend a few days in a house as horrible as this—provided, of course, Ash gets locked up in her room and swathed from head to toe mummy fashion and I get to go and do everything I want. Just like in the old days with Dad.

And actually, the house was not so ugly as unused, empty, neglected. It was a large, brown, two-story thing, with an oddly shaped roof and tiny gables above the second-floor windows that came to peaks. Some of the windows were boarded over, but the two uncovered ones stared out at us like blind eyes. The house was silent, cold, and slimy, even on a warm, sunny day in late June. Wait'll David and Berry find out I'll be staying here this year, and not at the McCarthy farm. Why, out here we're practically sitting on Black Lake!

And then two things happened at once. Cory realized how hurt my dad was and Dorothea Harrower, a friend of my father's and the real estate agent from Langtown, came tearing up the road in her jeep.

Cory touched my father's arm and breathed a deep lungful of country air. Then she smiled and said, "This is going to be absolutely heaven this summer, and our own private retreat."

My father relaxed. "Really? You honestly like it, B.C.?"

B.C. Baby Cory—the endearment my father uses. I gagged. Baby Cory was at least thirty-eight and a solid-looking aerobics nut.

"Oh, yes," said Cory. "I honestly do."

While they were exchanging these yucky honeymoon glances, Dorothea Harrower screeched to a halt and tumbled out of the jeep. She hurried up the overgrown path, jingling keys as she walked.

"Dotty," my father said and beamed at her. They hugged each other and then Mrs. Harrower spied me. I tried to pull back, but no good. In seconds, I was cooed over by and crushed against Langtown's sole actress and self-proclaimed "white" witch.

"Oh, Mikey!" she cried, jabbing me with a dangling parrot earring. "How you've grown!"

I heard Ash snicker behind me and pulled away, embarrassed. Geez. It's bad enough being treated like a baby, especially when you're eleven, but to suffer the cruelest indignity of all—Mikey. Only Mrs. Harrower called me that.

"M.J.," my father said quickly. "We call him M.J., Dot."

M.J. for Michael Joseph.

"Well, I'll try to remember that," she said. My father nudged Cory and Ash forward and introduced them. More hugs and squeals and "Welcome to Langtown." Finally, Mrs. Harrower calmed down enough to produce the keys to the house.

"Who owns this place, anyway?" my father asked, as we all trooped up to the front door. Miss Prep Princess tried to get in front of me, but I subtly maneuvered into the best position.

Mrs. Harrower inserted the key and struggled with the rusty lock. "I thought I told you," she said. "Why, it was my sister, Hetty. She absolutely loved this place at one time, but, well, she had to leave. She just couldn't live here anymore."

"Why? What happened?" asked Ash in her gravelly boy's voice.

"But my dears, don't you know?" Mrs. Harrower grinned naughtily at us. "You mean, no one's told you . . . ?"

"Told us *what?*" My father jiggled his suitcase, the dumb flute case, and the box of Ash's stuffed toys impatiently.

"Why, the house is haunted. I could swear to that on my reputation as a real witch."

Haunted.

For just a moment, the brilliant June sun slid behind a cloud and I felt cool standing there on the porch. Mrs. Harrower's twinkly blue eyes took on a sinister slant, as if she had just placed a curse on us.

But that was nonsense. This was a butterscotch-warm summer day in a sleepy country spot and Dorothea Harrower was a harmless, batty woman who thought she was a witch. And that was all there was to it.

But my father had dropped the suitcase, stuffed animals, and flute case with a thud. And Ash's zombie face had quivered into life. So, I thought, Her Iceberg Highness has fears after all.

But her next words squelched my hopes.

"Wow," she breathed. "Ghosts."

It was not said in dainty, girlish horror, but in ghoulish anticipation.

"Ashley," Cory said in a short tone. She kind of glared at my father, who managed a laugh.

"All right, Dot, you've had your fun. The joke's over, though."

"Really, Mark," said Mrs. Harrower, widening her eyes innocently. "This isn't a joking matter."

"Now, Mrs. Harrower—er—Dorothea," interrupted Cory, "surely you don't want to scare the children."

Ashley snorted and for once I agreed with her. It seemed that my father and Cory were the nervous ones, and not the "children." Of course, much as I would have loved to get better acquainted with a supernatural being, I really didn't believe in ghosts. I laughed at camp fire stories when other boys around me shivered, and the only time I got scared in horror movies was when I realized I wouldn't have enough money to buy both the big tub of hot buttered popcorn and the hot dog and soda.

But when the crash came from inside the locked house, I surprised myself by jumping nearly a foot off the floor. So much for nerves of steel.

"What was that?" Cory asked my dad. Her fingers had tightened on his arm.

"Oh my gosh," Ash said in a small voice. "This is too much."

My father held up his hands. "Calm down, everybody.

Now, Dotty, if you could get that infernal door open, I think we'll learn that the Slime That Ate Langtown has not really paid us a call."

I giggled and so did Ash. At least she had a sense of humor behind all that droopy blonde hair. But Cory wasn't smiling and neither was Mrs. Harrower or my father.

The door had finally been opened and we stampeded into the house, my father and Mrs. Harrower leading the way.

"Shh." My dad suddenly stopped and held up a hand.

We came to an abrupt halt in the semidarkness of the hall, breathing heavily, our hearts thumping. Well, mine was at any rate. And Cory's, too, I bet. For someone who looked as though she were in a shampoo commercial and did a thousand jumping jacks and sit-ups a day, she sure looked pale. Miss Hockey Stick U.S.A., however, stood in the center of the musty hallway, taking everything in without a flicker of an eyelash. Wasn't she scared of anything? I thought.

We all stood there, frozen, my stepmother clutching my father's arm, Mrs. Harrower squeezing her eyes shut as if communing with the atmosphere of the house.

"I sense," she whispered, fluttering her eyes, "yes, I sense a presence in there!"

She flung a hand out dramatically, and even before my father could say a word, we heard the sound of something rasping or grating. And it came from the direction in which she was pointing.

"Wha-what is it, Mark?" Cory said in a little-girl voice.

9

"Come on, let's find out!" Ash said, almost straining at the leash to meet whatever horror lurked in the house.

"No, Ashley, wait. I want to check this out alone. It might be a burglar. You stay here with your mother."

With a grumble, she subsided. Then she peeked at me through the curtain of her hair and gave me one of those funny you're-an-alien-from-another-planet-and-I-don't-understand-you-at-all looks. Geez, she was a pain. What did she expect me to do? Race after my father and help him tackle the horror or the intruder? Well, thanks but no thanks. If she wanted to die from a case of terminal macho, then let her. But I wanted to live to see my twelfth birthday. Or at least the big Phillies baseball game on July Fourth.

"Oh, Mark, be careful." Cory threw my dad another honeymoon look. He smiled grimly and tiptoed into what appeared to be the dining room/kitchen area of the house.

"Gee, Mrs. Harrower, what do you think's in there? A real ghost?" Ash whispered.

But Cory snapped, "Ashley Avis Lasker Garrett, you stop that nonsense this second!"

"Better a ghost than a burglar," I piped up and then we heard Dad give a shout and we all rushed in.

There stood my father in the dusty-looking kitchen. He was grinning and pointing at something on the floor. It was a jar of peanut butter and it would roll and then stop, almost by magic, on the tiled kitchen floor.

Cory peered at the jar. "That's what made the noise before? When it fell off the counter?"

"Apparently," he said and shrugged. "I take it this is our culprit."

"But what made it roll off the counter in the first place?" Ash asked. "And why does it keep moving now?"

My father squatted and ran his fingers over the tile. "The floor's uneven. And as for the crash, well, maybe a sharp gust of wind or . . ." But his voice trailed away as he stood up and examined the room. The only window not boarded up was over the sink, but that was nailed down.

"No, no, no." Mrs. Harrower sighed and looked at us as though we were misbehaving first graders. "Can't you see? The evidence is right there in front of you and you're blind. You're looking at windows and floors for logical, scientific explanations, but the real explanation is staring you right in the face."

"And that is?" my dad asked.

"Why, poltergeists," she said, in a quiet voice. "You've got yourself a poltergeist. And a peanut-butter-loving one, at that."

2

~~~~~~~~~

"Oh, wow," Ash started whispering beside me. "Oh, wow."

The girl was a nut, Grade A certified, no question about it. And the most annoying nut in the world. How could she fall for such a ridiculous statement so easily?

At least I kept my sanity. And so did my dad.

"Well, Dorothea," he said in this falsely cheerful voice, "that's very interesting. Yessiree, we're all mighty impressed. But if you'll excuse us now, we have a lot of unpacking to do."

One hand had gone under Mrs. Harrower's elbow, the other around her waist—he was trying to march her out of the kitchen and as far away from the "children's" fragile earshot as possible. But the lady wasn't buying any of his phony enthusiasm. She and my father had been friends for too many summers.

"Now, Mark Garrett, you listen to me," she said in a stern voice. "I know you think I've got bats in my belfry—

13

no, don't interrupt. I know you do from the expression on your face. Well, let me tell you, you're not the only one. Being the only real witch in this part of Bucks County can be very trying at times. No one believes a word you say. Of course, I get all the best parts in the plays at the little theater." She suddenly smiled. "They're all so afraid it might be true and I'll put a hex on them or something! Still, what I say about this house is not from my imagination, Mark. You must believe me. My sister Hetty felt it, too. I'm sure that's why she moved." She twisted her hands and gave us all a guilty look. "Oh, dear, I shouldn't have rented out her place to you, or anyone else for that matter, until I was sure it was empty! I just assumed the spirits wouldn't show themselves to disbelievers."

"But, Dorothea," Cory put in, "the spirits *haven't* shown themselves. Unless you call an old peanut butter jar a visitation."

"You don't know anything about poltergeists, do you?" Mrs. Harrower asked. "They're funny little things. Literally, the word means noisy spirits. And how true that is. You know you have a poltergeist when you hear loud thumpings in the house, or light bulbs suddenly explode, or your cups sail off a shelf for no good reason."

"But what causes all this weird stuff?" I asked. I couldn't help myself. I knew it was pure fantasy, but still, I was curious.

And yet the fountain of knowledge had dried up. That was strange. And what was even stranger, Mrs. Harrower caught my father's eye and shook her head slightly. Oh, it was subtle, *sneaky* subtle, but I caught it.

14

"M.J., Ash, run outside and start bringing in the suit-cases."

I knew it. The "children" were being excused just when the good stuff was being dished out.

"Ah, Dad . . ."

"Now. You, too, Ashley."

"Ah, Mom . . ."

"Go. Not another word."

We dawdled until we reached the hallway, then Ash put a finger to her lips and tiptoed very skillfully over the creaky floorboards, back to the kitchen. For someone who looked like a sleepy zombie half the time, she could really move. I shrugged, and made after her. No way was I going to let the Python Princess hear all the juicy stuff and not me.

We stopped outside the half-open kitchen door and pressed against the wall.

". . . and no one knows why," Mrs. Harrower was saying in a low voice, "but that's usually what it's centered on."

There was a sharp intake of breath from Cory. "But *children*? That's insane."

Children? Ash peered at me through the blonde veil and I peered back. This was really getting good! We stuck our heads closer to the door, banging them together in the process, the Two Stooges in the Haunted House. Then we heard Mrs. Harrower say, "The point of the whole thing is that in almost every case of poltergeists, the person through whom the poltergeist gets into the house is a young person, sometimes a child and sometimes a teen-

15

ager. And there's usually some tension or emotional trouble centered around the child."

"Well, then, that proves you're wrong," Cory said in a firm voice. "I know for certain this house has no poltergeists. There is absolutely not a tense or troubled bone in my daughter Ashley's body, or in my stepson M.J.'s."

Yeah, but what about the tension *between* them? I thought. And as if on cue, a cold little breeze swirled around my ankles, then seemed to slap me on my back as if to say, Bingo! You have just given the correct answer and may now pass Go. I rubbed my neck and eyed Ash, but she didn't so much as twitch or give the slightest shiver. Geez, she was as lifeless as a stale Hostess Twinkie and about as useful, too. And every time she slanted one of those glassy *Children of the Damned* stares my way, I felt like marching up to her mother and saying: "Here, no offense meant, it was a nice idea giving me a prepackaged sister and all that, but she's a little defective, if you know what I mean. And she's not what I would have chosen for a family member at all, so please exchange her or take her back and that new ten-speed racing bike will do fine for me instead."

At that, I started to giggle. Ash glared at me. Which only made it worse. The laugh swelled into a muffled combination of chortles and snickers and other silly noises, and that's when my darling stepsister, the Prep School Princess, thrust out tentacle fingers and pinched my arm. I yelped. I put out a hand to grab her, but only got a few

16

strands of yellow hair. I tugged anyway. Then she, in turn, yelped and before we knew it the door burst open, and my father and Cory were staring at us in horror.

"Ashley Avis!" Cory shouted. "Stop it at once!"

"Michael Joseph!" My dad chimed in, a fierce glint in his normally soft brown eyes. "You will kindly stop fighting this instant."

"She started it. . . ." I began.

"He did," Ash said angrily.

"That's enough!" my father said. "If you can't behave yourself, Michael, then you don't deserve to go to the Phillies game July Fourth."

"Oh, but Dad, we *always* go to the game July Fourth. It's a tradition. Something we always do every summer." I heard my voice wobble and hated it. But it was so unfair. Unfair! UNFAIR. And it was all Ashley's fault.

Behind us came the grating sound of the peanut butter jar. It rolled straight out of the kitchen into the dining room, the scene of the battle, where it came to a halt right at our feet.

We all looked at each other and then Mrs. Harrower coughed gently behind us. "You were saying about the tension level, Mrs. Garrett? But honestly, if anyone's got to be worried at all these next two weeks, I'd say it would be your peanut butter poltergeist."

Dorothea Harrower, better known now as Batty Dotty, had stirred up quite a storm in our family.

A sense of gloom hung over the house and unpacking

and settling in Saturday night was a quiet time for all of us, especially for me.

I was still smarting over my father's decision to call off our traditional July Fourth Phillies game. I couldn't believe it. My dad and I always went to both the opening day and July Fourth games. And I always wore my prized Phillies cap on these occasions. A number of Phillies greats had autographed it for me; whenever I was bugged about something, I stuck it on my head and wore it all over—indoors, outdoors, night or day. Once, on the night before a really big test, I wore it to bed. (I didn't pass the test, but the teacher allowed me to take it over because of the strange red marks around my hairline.)

Now that my dad had axed the baseball game, I jammed the cap on my head in protest. But deep down inside, somehow, someway, I knew I was going to get to that game. That, and my simmering feud with Ashley, was the only thing on my mind. Oh, we playacted "making up," but that was for our parents' sake. Ashley Avis Lasker Garrett was never going to be a friend of mine, not if I could help it. We were too different. Not because she was taller, stronger, and older than I was, but because she seemed so determined to get her own way. Nothing scared or bothered her. And that bothered me.

When we chose our rooms Saturday night, she asked for the downstairs bedroom. It was smaller than the bedroom upstairs, but it was situated right off the living room and close to the kitchen, perfect for midnight snack attacks. Plus it had its own bathroom and was far away from my father and Cory's master bedroom on the second floor. It was just right for me.

"Hey . . . !" I started to complain, and then fell silent. My father's eagle eye had shot me "the message."

"All right," I said tonelessly. "I guess I'm stuck with the room upstairs."

"But it's got a lovely view," Cory said quickly. "You can see the woods and part of the lake from the window."

"What can you do with a view?" I shrugged. "Microwave with it? Watch MTV with it? Take it to a baseball game?"

And with a loud martyr's sigh, I picked up my suitcase and trudged upstairs. This was turning out to be a hideous summer vacation and I wanted to be sure that everyone in the Garrett family knew exactly how I felt. So I slammed drawers and closet doors and had a great time pretending I was being tortured on the rack.

That was Day One of the supposedly fabulous vacation. Only thirteen more hideous days to go.

Day Two, Sunday, began gruesomely, but fooled me halfway through.

Right after a tense breakfast of glowering looks between Ashley and me, I asked my dad if I could see David and Berry DeRemer. The DeRemers owned the only coffee shop/boating place in Langtown and lived right off the Delaware River near town. I guessed it would take me about ten minutes to walk to their house.

My father poured himself another cup of coffee and

19

then gave me a wave. "Sure, go ahead. But take Ash with you. I bet she'd like to meet your friends."

The Alien Creature shot me another of those expressionless looks and I quivered into life.

"She doesn't want to tag along with me, Dad! She'd be bored. David's eleven and Berry's only nine. Minor league stuff in her book."

My dad's gimlet eyes impaled mine. "Why don't you ask her?"

"Uh, Ash, you wouldn't want to take a hike with me and meet these goofy friends of mine, kids really, no, almost babies."

The gravel pit voice spoke up. "Sure."

Sure? I could swear her lips were twitching, but I couldn't be certain under all that hair.

Grumbling under my breath, my cap jammed defiantly on my head, I walked out of the house without saying good-bye. Right behind me skipped Ash. Yeah, skipped. She was so happy because she knew she'd be torturing me on this beautiful summer morning. Who needed her along? And how would I explain her presence to David and Berry? We were used to being the Fearsome Threesome, and now this unwanted addition.

Fifteen minutes later I was the odd man out.

I couldn't believe how quickly it all happened. The first thing I knew I was greeting David and Berry in the big yard behind their father's coffee shop, and sullenly introducing Ash as quickly as I could. We had interrupted an informal batting practice. The next thing I knew my stepsister had commandeered the bat and was knocking out

20

hard-driving home-run balls, one right after the other! David stared at her, openmouthed, while Berry scurried to retrieve the balls.

"Hey!" David yelled. "Teach me to do that!"

"Me, too!" Berry cried. She was munchkin-sized, and pipsqueak-voiced. Teaching Berry to connect with the ball, let alone hit home runs, would have been a miracle. But Berry sensed a celebrity when she saw one.

"Aw, let's not fool around here," I said quickly. "Let's go to the lake."

No one wanted to go.

I sat on the grass, watching, until I couldn't take any more. David was chattering away to Ash like they were bosom buddies from the dinosaur age, and—stranger than strange!—she was chattering back to him. I couldn't believe how animated she had become. What happened to the sleepy zomboid? And even Berry, a loyal member of the Fearsome Threesome, was bouncing up and down next to Ash and running eagerly after every ball.

"Who needs them?" I said disdainfully and got to my feet. There's plenty around here to keep me occupied. But Langtown on a hot, lazy day moved along like a ninety-year-old caterpillar. And it was so quiet that I could hear the sheep three meadows over chewing their grass.

A day and a quarter down, I thought. Twelve and three-quarters more to go.

But hey! Who's counting?

3

Sunday night came and went. Not a peep. Not a rattle. Not a creature was stirring in our spooky old house.

Not even a poltergeist.

Mrs. Harrower's predictions failed to materialize, and nothing more was heard rolling around in the kitchen or felt prickling up the goose bumps on my neck. Even the trusty peanut butter jar stayed upright and obedient in its place of honor on the kitchen shelf.

Maybe the "noisy spirit" was taking a siesta or off at some normal household in the neighborhood, playing couch potato and watching all the good shows on TV. There was certainly nothing to keep it at our place. Dorothea Harrower's sister, Hetty, may have fled in horror from the house's ghostly vibrations, but she remembered to take the TV set with her when she left.

That meant we had such exciting home entertainment options as playing Monopoly and Crazy Eights and reading aloud from Charles Dickens' *Great Expectations*, one of my father's favorite books. Two other ideas brought up, but vehemently squelched by me, were doing calisthenics with Cory or listening to Ash practice the flute.

As you can see, the Garrett family was really moving in the fast lane on this vacation.

Monday morning, after another strained breakfast, my dad settled into the little back porch area with his paints and paper. He worked as a commercial artist and often took assignments from publishers to illustrate covers for their books. This project was very important, he told us, because it had to be sketched and painted before the week was out. Deadlines again, even on his time off. But that was the kind of job he had. Cory wasn't thrilled about this but managed to keep a smiling face. Knowing her, she'd use the time to try out different recipes and work in more aerobic routines. And Ash? She grimaced and said she might as well practice the flute. I was surprised she had the strength in her wrists to hold up an instrument, let alone play Tiddlywinks, after her Mickey Mantle exhibition yesterday. But then, an alien being from another planet lived in her body.

It was nearing eleven, and I was slowly going crazy with boredom, when Cory popped her head outside and asked if I wanted to help with the grocery shopping. The book I was reading hadn't captured my interest, so I scrambled off the grass and jumped into the car.

An hour and two full grocery bags later, we were loading the car when the resident witch came striding into view.

"Mikey! I mean, M.J. and Mrs. Garrett!" Mrs. Harrower yodeled, catching sight of us.

"Oh, no," Cory groaned softly behind me. After the poltergeist talk on Saturday, Dorothea Harrower was not one of my stepmother's favorite people. But she plastered an overbright smile on her face and returned Mrs. Harrower's wave.

"And how is everything working out for you? I mean, have you heard any more from our, ahem, little 'friend'?" Mrs. Harrower lowered her voice and looked cautiously up and down the street just like in a spy thriller.

"Little friend?" Cory said in a cool voice. "I'm sorry, I don't know what you're talking about."

"The poltergeist!" I piped up. "The peanut-butter-loving one." And I laughed. Mrs. Harrower laughed too, in that dramatic actressy way of hers, flinging her head back and shaking from side to side. But Cory tossed her short blonde hair and set her lips together.

"I think you're both out of your minds, personally," she said. "But go ahead, laugh about it if you want. I'd rather have you treat it like a joke than take it seriously."

"Oh, but I do, I do," Mrs. Harrower assured her, wiping at her eyes. "And you will too, my dear. Just a few more nights in that house and I guarantee it. Well, I must run. I have to show a house to a client in Erwinna. But the boring thing is, this house *isn't* haunted. Ciao."

And as Mrs. Harrower sailed away, Cory muttered, "Ciao to you, too. Oh, that woman drives me crazy with her talk about 'ghostly vibrations' and 'little friends.' "

Before I could defend Mrs. Harrower, I heard a shout and then David raced to the curb on his bike and braked within inches of my foot.

"Hey, M.J., what are you up to?"

"Not much."

"Want to go fishing tomorrow morning at the lake?"

"Yeah, sure. Great."

"Okay. I'll bring the rods. How's six-thirty sound?"

"Gruesome, but let's do it!"

"Yeah. Oh, bring Ash, too."

I felt my smile freeze and a scowl replace it. "Aw, she wouldn't want to do that." Cory had shoved the last bag in the trunk and was now chatting with some neighbors in the street. She couldn't hear me, but I lowered my voice anyway. "Come on, David. She's a girl. Think of how she'll moan and groan when she has to get up at the crack of dawn. Forget that. Wait until she has to deal with the worms."

He gave me a puzzled look. "Are you kidding? Ash? She's so tough she'd probably be able to stick an eel on a hook and not squirm."

"Tough? You think she's tough?"

"Yeah. I do."

"What? The Clint Eastwood/Conan the Barbarian of Langtown?"

"No, but close."

"I bet you anything Ash isn't tough. I bet you anything it's just a big act she puts on."

"Oh, yeah?" David said. "Prove it."

My heart was pounding as I thought rapidly. Not only

26

was my honor at stake, and also my special friendship with David, but also the opportunity to get to that July Fourth Phillies game, if I played my cards right. Cory had wrapped up her conversation and was getting into the car, so I said as fast as I could, "I bet you I can scare the pants off of Ash, so that she demands, no, she begs to get out of Langtown before July Fourth."

"That's crazy. You can't."

"I can."

"Can't. Nothing scares her."

"Wanna bet?"

"We'd have to be betting on something pretty good." David bit his lip, then eyed me and snapped his fingers. "I got it! I'll take you on if you bet me your Phillies baseball cap."

I stared at him in horror and made an instinctive move toward my head.

"Relax, it's still there." David grinned. "But won't be there much longer, if you go ahead with this crazy bet."

That did it. I stuck out my hand and David whistled.

"You're really going to do it? You're ready to shake on it?"

I nodded.

"This'll be the easiest bet I've ever won," David said, then thought for a second before shaking. "Wait a sec. What do I have to give you if I lose?"

"Nothing. Absolutely nothing. Except for letting me say I told you so, a hundred times to your face."

"You're sick, you know that?" He hesitated, then hurriedly shook hands as Cory called, "Let's go, M.J. Your father's going to be ravenous by the time we get home."

I jumped in the car, a triumphant grin on my face.

Because I had just hit upon the perfect plan to turn Ashley Garrett, Her Iceberg Highness, into a whimpering mass of cowardice.

And Batty Dotty had given me the idea.

I was to become the Peanut Butter Poltergeist.

I was going to terrify Ashley into begging her mother to leave Langtown—and the creepy old house that seemed to have it in for her.

If I had any qualms at all about playing such a mean trick on my stepsister, they vanished after what happened Tuesday morning.

It was early. I was sleepy, but then bright eyed and wide awake when I remembered why I had set my alarm: the fishing date with David. I jumped out of bed, threw on old clothes, and then tiptoed carefully down the creaky stairs. I didn't want Cory to wake up and start playing mother, telling me what to wear or what to take if it rained or got too hot. I was rolling around the kitchen, throwing such delectable breakfast items as pickles and bananas and Oreo cookies into a paper bag, when I felt the back of my neck prickle. Something cool had just gusted into town. I realized how absolutely still the house was. And then I heard a sound. It was a cross between a moan and a death rattle and I jumped about a foot in the air before I wheeled around—and saw Ash. Making a weird monster face and holding her hands out in front of her like claws. Laughing at me like a low-I.Q. hyena.

"Geez!" I growled. "Pretty funny."

The monster face relaxed back into the normal sleep-walking one. "Sorry. But I couldn't help it. Your shoulders were halfway up to your neck like the Hunchback of Notre Dame. Did you think I was the ghost?"

I gave a nervous snort. She had hit too close to home. Ignoring the question as if it were beneath me, I finished jamming the Oreos into the bag. Ash stood there, watching my every movement with those weird eyeballs of hers. It gave me the creeps. I hurried into the hallway, intent on getting to the door, when I heard her voice behind me.

"Aren't you forgetting something?"

I turned and looked into those muddy brown eyes of hers, always impossible to read.

"What?"

She grinned and produced something from behind her back. My baseball cap! I reached for it. She pulled it away.

"Hey!"

It's a little difficult trying to grab something away from a moving Empire State Building, but I tried. Oh, I tried. Moments later, humiliated, my face flushed, I gave up. Is that how King Kong felt when the dive-bomber planes started zapping him?

I gave a disdainful snort as if the cap meant nothing to me, picked up the breakfast bag, and opened the door with as much dignity as I could muster.

The gravel pit voice shot out, "Why's the stupid cap so important to you, anyway?"

"Why's the stupid stuffed animal collection so important to you, anyway?" I shot back.

She didn't react the way I thought she would, just stared at me in silence. Then her lips twitched.

"Where are you going?"

"Out."

"Out where?"

"Just out."

I didn't want to tell her, for fear she'd say she wanted to tag along. If I couldn't get my hat from her, I certainly couldn't stop her from following me to the lake. I sidled out the door.

"Yeah, well, have fun *out*," she said, "fishing."

That spun me around. "Well, hey, how did you—I mean, that's not where I'm going."

"Oh, getting up this early to go bird-watching or something?"

"Well, no, but—"

"Give up, M.J. I know all about it. I heard you ask your father last night if you could go."

"We were outside, for pete's sake, playing catch! What were you doing, hanging out the window, eavesdropping?"

Ash looked startled, then tightened her lips. When she spoke, her voice had managed to descend far below the gravel pit level to a subterranean coal mine.

"That's not what I was doing." She practically spit out the words. "I was on my way out to join you, as a matter of fact, but, well, I changed my mind. Is that a crime?"

30

Geez, women! Or should I say, geez, a space alien posing as a girl? Here I was, all set to be mad, but how could I be when she hung her head so dejectedly and blinked her eyes and looked vulnerable. Well, what could I do? My conscience tugged at me. *Go ahead,* it whispered, *ask her to go fishing with you. She's a real live human being, not a reptilian robot.*

I swallowed, took a deep breath, and heard myself issue the invitation. There was a momentary glow in my heart as my conscience cheered, *Good boy!* But everything was ruined when Ash opened her mouth.

"Hey, thanks, nerdman. C'mon, I'll race you to the lake and winner gets the best fishing rod. And I bet I catch more fish than you!"

And with a toss of that stringy yellow hair, she was off and running, a blur of arms and legs, my cap in her hand.

"Hey!" I called. "Hey! Wait up!"

I stumbled out the door after her and made a vow. The Peanut Butter Poltergeist was going to make its very first appearance that night or my name wasn't Michael Joseph Garrett.

4

"Why, whatever's wrong with your appetite, M.J.?" Cory said to me at the dinner table. "You've barely touched a thing on your plate."

"No, I'm fine, see? I'm eating."

I picked up a spear of broccoli and put it in my mouth, smiling at Cory and chewing with greater enthusiasm than I felt. But she still shot a puzzled look at my plate.

"Yes, but your fish. You haven't taken a bite."

Across the table, Ash coughed and our eyes met. Beneath the curtain of hair, I could detect a gleam of victory in those zombie eyes. Victory because the glory had all been hers today, in front of David, in front of my dad. Not only had Ash beaten me to the lake and taken the good fishing rod, but guess who caught the big, BIG trout everyone had oohed and aahed over? I had caught something, too: part of an inner tube and a fish the size of a minnow, but I was trying to forget.

"Heavens, B.C., come look at this!" my dad had cried when we straggled back to the house late in the morning.

Cory dashed from the living room in her leotard and leg warmers, a huge grin splitting her face at her daughter's prize.

"Guess I know what we'll be eating tonight," my father boomed, proudly throwing an arm around Ash's shoulders. "Jaws Three's second cousin."

Ha, ha. Everyone laughed, but I was feeling out of it and jealous again. All this fuss over Ashley's catch. You'd think she had captured and manicured a Bengal tiger, rather than hooked a helpless fish.

Well, no way was I going to inflate her already Goodyear-Blimp–sized head and congratulate her. And no way was I going to take one bite of her crummy fish. So there I sat at the dining room table, pushing the food around on my plate and trying to avoid Ash's eyes. It wasn't only pride that kept me from eating. It was anticipation and excitement. Because that very evening I was planning my very first appearance as the ghost! I couldn't wait to play my little tricks. I couldn't wait to see Ash's tough guy exterior crumble.

I looked at my watch: seven o'clock. Just a few more hours and the Peanut Butter Poltergeist would appear.

A little after midnight I was ready. This country living was so slow we all went to bed about ten. I put my ear against the door of the master bedroom—all quiet, except for the light snores of my father. Safe there. I glided downstairs, clutching my flashlight and a small clock and feeling like a cat burglar. It had been warm but cloudy earlier, and now a heavy wind had picked up. The sound effects were eerie, with the tree branches tapping the windows and the old place creaking like a rocking chair gone bananas. But I was glad for the noise. It would cover up any sounds I might make.

Still, I had to admit my heart was beating a little fast as I made my way into the dark downstairs hallway. Dark? Try three layers of swathing deep around a mummy. I flicked the flashlight on and kept the glow covered with my hand as I made my way to the kitchen. Just before I reached the door I heard a sharp tap.

"Whoa, Batman," I whispered, and froze for what seemed like twenty minutes. Actually, it was more like a minute and when I got up my couage, I sort of danced into the kitchen doing an imitation kung-fu kick and trying to look like a vicious undercover cop. Nothing happened. No one jumped out at me. I played the flashlight all over the room, but saw nothing. Then the tap came again, and I realized what it was. The screen on the back-porch door was knocking in the wind. So much for things that go bump in the night. That was going to be *my* department.

Grinning to myself, I placed the flashlight and clock on the counter, and then got to work on the canisters. What had Mrs. Harrower said? That poltergeists were noisy, mischievous spirits? Heck, I could be as mischievous as the best of them.

Quietly, oh so quietly, I took the lids off all the canisters and spilled some flour and sugar and tea bags on the floor and cabinet. Not too much to make clearing up a problem, but enough to say a spirit was there. Then I pulled open the drawers beside the sink and quickly took out knives, spoons, and forks, which I placed in the sink itself and also on the floor. I wound up the small old alarm clock I had found earlier in the back of my bedroom dresser, and set the alarm to go off for nine-thirty the next morning. Then I placed it inside the stove. That left the pictures on the wall to deal with, and then, finally, Ash's room.

I tiptoed into the dining room and took down the two old-fashioned oil paintings that hung there. With a sharp serrated knife, I frayed and half cut the wires attached to the frames. Then I carefully rehung the pictures. With any luck, the paintings would crash to the floor sometime within the next twenty-four hours, hopefully when Ash was around.

Her room next, I said to myself, trying to cover my nervousness. What if she woke up and found me moving objects in her room? The game would be up, and she would have me in her unearthly power for the rest of her life, to pummel, pound, or order about as much as she wished. No, I vowed, I'd be as silent as a mouse. She wouldn't hear me.

I made my way extracautiously to her bedroom and opened her door as silently as I could. Once I got inside, I stood in the darkness, straining to hear and to see. Yeah, she was dead to the world, I thought. Lying flat on her stomach, a frog in men's pajamas, her long hair fanned out over the pillow, and small gusts of breathing to indicate a deep sleep. So space aliens doze off, too. How interesting.

Feeling a little bolder, I advanced into her room, and then almost bumped into a rocking chair. I was glad I did. I could make out in the darkness that it held all her dopey stuffed animals, little snouts and beaks and bills poking up at me. There. I'd start there. With rapid movements I collected the toys and then silently strewed them all over the floor, on the windowsill, by her closet. I walked to the bureau and felt around. Bingo. Within seconds I had moved her perfectly arranged comb and brush set, and then placed all her hair barrettes on the bottom of the coverlet. I quickly stepped into her closet and half pulled some shirts off the hangers, then switched pairs of her shoes around. There, that would do it.

After I was done, I stepped back and appraised the scene. Really, it was quite good. Even in the dark and squinting, I could tell that a mischievous, playful spirit had been there. Not destructive. Not malicious. Just Casper the Friendly Ghost.

Ash suddenly blew a bubble, muttered something inaudible, and I froze. But the seconds ticked by and she didn't wake up. Saved again, I thought. My heart thudding, I hurried out of her room and tiptoed up the stairs. The Peanut Butter Poltergeist's work was done. Now all I had to do was go to sleep and wait until morning for the family's reaction.

A muffled shriek woke me early the next morning. The Python Princess had just gotten her first taste of the midnight visitor.

And judging from the noises next door, Cory and my father would be seeing the work of the poltergeist, too. I jumped out of bed and dashed into the hallway just as

they ran out the door, looking sleepy and worried at the same time.

"What in blazes is going on here?" my dad exclaimed, casting a bleary but irritated eye my way. "Were you making that racket?"

I held up my hands and played innocent. "Hey, don't look at me. I just woke up."

"I told you it was a cat," Cory said to my father, but just at that moment, unearthly wails pierced the air.

"Ashley!" Cory cried. "My baby!"

Pulling at her robe, she ran down the stairs, my father and I in hot pursuit. "Oh boy," I muttered under my breath, "oh boy, this is going to be fun!" Then I forced my twitching lips to be still and with a perfectly puzzled expression followed my father and Cory into Ash's bedroom.

It was not a pretty picture. My stepsister was on her hands and knees, long hair hanging over her eyes, frantically collecting all her precious stuffed toys. Every five seconds or so, she'd emit this hoarse wail. When she looked up and saw me, her muddy brown eyes flashed.

"You!" she cried. "You—you baby-faced creep!" Then she hurled a furry missile at me.

"Hey! What did I do?"

The stuffed toys kept coming. I held my hands in front of my face, not only for protection but to hide a grin.

"Now, Ashley Avis, just stop that! Stop that this minute!" Cory stepped forward, and Ash threw her a hostile look before subsiding. Then she jumped up and flung her hand out.

"Look at this room! Go on, just look! Do you think I did this, Mom?"

Three pairs of eyes automatically swiveled around her bedroom. Two stared incredulously, one stared in masked pride. Geez, I was brilliant. I was so brilliant Albert Einstein could take a correspondence course from me. The room was a shambles, but wait until they saw the kitchen!

"Why, I—I don't understand," Cory said in a faint voice. "What happened?"

"What happened?" Ash impaled me with an icicle stare. "Tell them what happened, nerdlebrain. Since you know, tell them."

"I don't know!" I burst out. "I didn't do anything! I mean it. Why would I creep around your silly room, playing with your stuffed animals and your clothes? Gee, I hate stuffed animals and I sure can't fit into your clothes."

It sounded convincing to me. My father peered intently into my face, which I made as cherubic as possible, then looked across at Cory with a helpless shrug. She gave a puzzled shrug back. And even Ash couldn't answer that one.

The flare in my stepsister's eyes had gone out, but she still said in a dull voice, "I don't care. I don't care. *You* must have done it last night, because I sure didn't."

"Well, it wasn't me. Honest, Ash." I bent over and began helping her pick up the animals. At first she ignored my outstretched hand, but then, with a sniff, coldly took the toys from me.

Behind me, Cory gave a frightened cough. "Mark, you

don't think, I mean, we couldn't have had, well, a *bur-glar?"*

The last word was whispered, but I caught it plain enough. Oh, great, I thought. I go to all this trouble and now my stepmother thinks a burglar did it, not a poltergeist. But they hadn't seen the kitchen yet.

"No, B.C., I don't think so," my father replied, but I could sense his confusion.

"I'll start looking around," I piped up, and headed straight for the kitchen. The sight was truly a shocker in the daylight, and I didn't have to fake my excitement when I shouted, "Dad! Cory! Come in here, fast!"

When everyone rushed in, pandemonium broke out. Cory squealed, putting her hands to her face in horror. My father stood in the middle of the kitchen with a grim look on his face.

"If it is burglars . . ." he said slowly, but then opened the cookie jar and extracted several bills. "The money's still here. I don't get it."

Ash forgot to pout as she skipped over to the back door. She fiddled around with the handle and cried, "Dad! Look! The door's still locked."

Every time she calls my father that, I grimace. He's my father, not hers. At least not by blood. But it pleased him to know she felt that way, and I also knew Cory was still waiting and secretly hoping I'd start calling her Mom, instead of Cory. Right now it didn't feel right, so I didn't.

"And Cory, look over here." I led the way to the windows, the screens tightly latched to the frames.

The four of us stood in the middle of a sugar-and-flour-coated floor, eyeing the mess, thinking. I knew my father and Cory didn't buy the ghost theory, but Ash was only too willing to suspend her disbelief, if only to brag to her admiring circle of friends how she arm wrestled a spook over her summer vacation. Let her begin to believe. She was the one I had to convince, anyway.

Cory picked a spoon up off the floor in a daze. "Mark?" she whispered. "You don't think . . . ?"

"Think what?"

She didn't say a word, just mutely nodded in the direction of the kitchen shelf—and the peanut butter jar.

My father threw back his head and laughed. "Come on, honey! Now you're starting to sound like Dotty Harrower. I admit this has me puzzled, but everything's got a logical explanation, and if I really think about it—hey! Wait a second!" He snapped his fingers and grinned. "You know that storm we had last night? Maybe the high winds caused the house to shift and disturbed the shelving and made the tins fall off. I bet that's it. I'm going to call Carl DeRemer right now and see if he experienced the same thing at his place."

I was about to point out that silverware doesn't leap out of closed drawers, but the scared look in Cory's eyes stopped me. My father got Carl DeRemer on the phone and held a brief conversation with him. The upshot was that no earthquake or windstorm had disturbed the DeRemer house. My father listened, and rubbed his jaw.

"Say, Carl, just as a favor to me, could you stop out

41

here after work tonight, say around eight? I'd like you to check this out."

The two men concluded their plans and then my dad hung up. He looked at our glum faces and managed a laugh.

"Hey, come on, this isn't the end of the world. The vacation's not over because we've got a faulty foundation in this fun house. Now, I don't know about the rest of you, but I'm wide awake and I'm ravenously hungry and I'm just itching to make us some waffleburgers the size of an elephant's toe. Ash, you ever have my infamous waffleburgers?"

The Preppie Princess wrinkled her nose. "El grosso."

"They are not, you'll love them," my father announced, keeping a straight face. "M.J. can attest to that. But first, I think we need to clean up this kitchen. The chef can't concoct his delicacies if his concentration is disturbed. Poltergeists, what a laugh."

He shot an amused glance at Cory, who colored faintly, then giggled. Within an hour or so, the whole house was returning to normal, when the Peanut Butter Poltergeist struck again. First, the paintings I had messed with crashed to the floor and then, two seconds later, after we had all jumped up, the alarm clock went off with a screech inside the oven.

And that, I thought smugly, was only the beginning.

5

My plan was working beautifully.

After the scary and unexplained events of the morning, Ash walked around all agitated. She was like the title of that play, *Cat on a Hot Tin Roof*. Every least noise or harmless sound in the house triggered off a banshee wail.

"Relax," my dad kept reassuring her. "There's nothing spooky about what's happened. Carl DeRemer will tell you that. He's into carpentry and construction and I bet he can pinpoint what's wrong with this place the minute he gets here. And it'll be a physical reason, not a supernatural one."

Although my dad said all this with a perfectly serious, straight face, his wriggling eyebrows revealed his uncertainty. How could he explain away an alarm clock suddenly going off and scaring everyone to death? So even my father was having doubts, and poor Cory walked around mumbling that she didn't want to get gray hairs on her honeymoon.

Things were falling into place nicely.

Carl DeRemer was coming over at eight o'clock that evening, a perfect witness to convince. David and Berry's father was the slowest talking, least emotional man I knew, calm, placid, like the cows that grazed just north of his boating place. Nothing ruffled his feathers. And I knew any talk of ghosts or goblins would be laughable to him. So putting on a really effective poltergeist trick might stop Mr. DeRemer in his unflappable tracks—and further frighten Ash. But it had to be good. It had to be dynamite.

I put on my thinking cap and spent half of the afternoon plotting out the next move. When I was finished, I knew I had a winner. Einstein, I crowed to myself, time to take a bow.

Somehow I got through dinner and managed to eat. I forced myself to talk to Ash, even though she peered at me through her curtain of hair with suspicion. It was hard going, because at some point during the day she had regained her insufferable confidence and sense of macho. The tough guy was back in place. The scared little girl was gone. And she laughed with my father over talk of a ghost.

"Ah," I said to myself in my best imitation of a war movie bad guy, "ve haf vays of making space creatures squeal!"

Carl DeRemer rang our doorbell a little before eight. Everyone went to greet him, and then we heard a yodeling sound coming up the walk. We knew that voice.

"Yoohoo, Mark and Cora Lynn!" cried Mrs. Harrower, striding up the steps to our porch and waggling her fingers. "I don't mean to barge in, but when I overheard Carl mentioning your little, ahem, 'trouble' this morning at the store, why, I just had to come over and see for myself. After all, this is my sister's house and I feel responsible for you."

Dramatic Batty Dotty. So perfect for my stunt this evening. Cory flinched beside me, but opened the door and welcomed her in true hostessy fashion.

While everyone headed for the kitchen, I darted into Ash's bedroom. There I hurriedly tied a nearly invisible thread around the bottom of a china vase on her dresser. Then I trailed the long thread with me, keeping my fingers inside my pocket. But a sharp tug from me, and the vase would seemingly fly through the air, as if unaided.

Step One of the operation went smoothly. Step Two would be a little more difficult to pull off. I had to get Ash inside her bedroom before Carl DeRemer and Mrs. Harrower left.

I sidled into the kitchen as if I had been there the whole while and came up behind Ash. While the grown-ups were taking measurements and talking seriously, I tapped my stepsister on the arm.

"I hope you're not getting any bright ideas about showing off for company by playing your flute."

Always contrary, she took the bait. "Why? Would it bother you?"

I shrugged. "Not me. I'm used to hearing the screeching sound of cats fighting."

With an angry squeal that brought everyone's head around, Ash took off and slammed into her bedroom.

45

"Whatever is going on with her?" Cory said, and just at that moment, hurriedly turning my back, I reeled in the thread as fast as I could. *Bingo! Bam! Crash!* We all heard something hit the floor and shatter.

"What in the world . . .?" My father exclaimed.

I zipped into Ash's room, anxious to remove the damaging evidence. Ash was standing bolt upright, her mouth open, a zombie expression on her face. She was too shocked to notice my crablike motions over the broken vase or my removing a thread.

"It . . . flew," she mumbled. "Right at me! It flew!"

I stood up as the others rushed in. One look at a dazed Ash and then the pieces of the broken vase, and the shouting started.

"All right, young lady, what happened in here? Did you knock that vase over?"

Ash cut off her mom. "It came off the dresser at me, like someone or something was throwing it! No, honest, Mom, I mean it! The vase just flew."

Cory blew out a long breath. "Next you'll be telling me the poltergeist did it! Now look, Ashley, don't be scared to admit you broke that vase. We can pay Dorothea whatever it cost and she'll tell her sister it was an accident —"

"No, it wasn't!" Ash interrupted, her voice little more than a whisper. "I would tell you if I broke it, but I didn't. I never touched the thing. I wasn't even near it! It came hurtling off the dresser and smashed on the floor. It scared me!" She shivered and even I had to admit it sounded frightening. If I hadn't known it was all my doing, I would be a quivering mass of jellyfish right about now.

Cory looked hard into Ash's face, but Ash just stared fiercely back at her.

"Ashley Avis . . . ?"

"I mean it, Mom! I didn't do it!"

"Well . . ." Cory flapped her hands in confusion and turned to my father. "She's not lying to me, Mark. I know my daughter."

Mrs. Harrower edged her way into this touching scene and peered over my shoulder at the shattered vase. "Of course she's not lying," Mrs. Harrower said with a glint in her eyes. "Why should she? This is a perfect example of a poltergeist manifestation, just like what happened in your kitchen last night."

From the door, Mr. DeRemer cleared his throat. "Now Dot, that hasn't been proved yet."

He took a pipe from his pocket and rolled it around in his hands and we all assumed a long lecture would follow. But then Mr. DeRemer scratched his head and subsided into silence. So much for a rebuttal from that corner.

"Now, Ashley, you told me that things were moved around in your bedroom last night?" Mrs. Harrower asked. "And no other room was disturbed except for the kitchen? And now a vase flies off a dresser and in whose room does this occur?"

My father began to say something, but thought better of it. Cory gave a sniff and took Ash into her arms.

"I don't care what you say. My daughter is no poltergeist!"

"Of course, *she's* not," Mrs. Harrower replied. "But there's no denying there's one living in this house, and it's the most exciting thing to happen in Langtown since Edna May Berkle ran off with the UPS man back in 1968!"

The next morning I totally stepped out of character.

I made a friendly overture to Ash and invited her to go with me to David and Berry's house. She looked at me with an I-don't-get-you-at-all expression and hesitated. I sensed she still had her doubts about me even though she didn't really believe I was the poltergeist. I was not topping the charts of her "One Hundred People I Have Known and Loved." But the invitation tempted her. She was a bundle of nerves after the past night and didn't want to be alone. Of course she'd have to be knocked on the head first by a lacrosse stick before admitting it.

"I don't know, M.J.," she said, trying to show how cool and indifferent she was. "I might have other plans for this morning."

"What, play the flute? Wash out your socks? Give the little stuffed animals a French lesson?"

"No, as a matter of fact, Charlotte Devlin asked me to go shopping with her and her mother in Flemington."

"Charlotte Devlin? You mean the fourteen-year-old wrestler down the hill who tries to look like a girl? You'd seriously consider taking your life in your hands to go out in public with someone like that?"

My father walked in at that moment and laughed. "As a matter of fact, I introduced Charlotte to Ashley. She's a

49

nice girl and it would be good for your sister to make some friends of her own in Langtown."

I'd have agreed, but not then. Not at that date and not at the stage of my plan where I almost had the Python Princess primed to run from the house.

"Well, that's too bad," I said, peering down at my fingernails with great interest. "Because David was trying to set up a baseball game. He specifically wanted Ash as captain of his team. But if she can't make it, if she'd rather ooh and aah at lipstick shades in a store with a female impersonator, then I guess I'll take her place."

I sighed, adjusted my baseball cap, and made for the door. Ash caught up with me in two steps.

"Hey, wait! I can do something with Charlotte later. I want to play ball."

I had her. I had hooked the fish. Ash could never pass up the opportunity to show off, especially in front of my friends.

"Just a second," my father said. "Can you be back here by noon, Ashley? I'd like you to sit for me while I do the last-minute artwork for the book jacket. The deadline's tomorrow, so I could really use your help."

"Me? Pose?" It was almost a squeal, and I recoiled. Ugh. "Sure, Dad, I'll come back in time for that!"

Of course she would, I thought, mentally patting myself on the back. Because I'd make her. Correction: The Peanut Butter Poltergeist would make her. I had another trick planned and this one was a winner.

When David opened the door, he smiled at Ash, but gave me a tiny frown.

"I hope you know what you're doing," he whispered, leading us down to his basement. "It sounds so crazy."

"Trust me."

Poor innocent Ash was chattering away to David as he handed her the baseball bats and gloves. She had no idea that in the next few seconds the poltergeist would pay her another visit. When their backs were turned, I pulled out my secret ammunition: a squirt gun! Then I crossed my fingers as I shot hard streams of water directly at the exposed light bulb dangling from the ceiling. I had asked David to turn it on a half hour before we got there so it would be good and hot.

The impact of the cold water caused an explosion that sent even me back and plunged the room into darkness. I quickly hid the gun in my back pocket.

Ash shrieked and I heard scuffling noises. Then a light appeared. David had found a flashlight. He shot it my way and I kept my face expressionless.

"Ash, are you all right?" I peered into the blackness and heard what sounded like a muffled sniff.

"Hey, c'mon. It's nothing to be scared of. The light bulb blew, that's all. I mean, it's not like the poltergeist followed you here and—"

"Oh, stop it! Don't be such a nerdbrain!" she exploded. "If I have to hear one more thing about poltergeists or spirits or ghosts I'll scream. Now come on, I came here to play baseball, so let's do it!"

And with a determined grunt, she made her way to the steps and hurriedly climbed them.

"Boy, oh boy, are you in for trouble." David whistled.

51

He came up close to me and flashed the light on his face so I could see his smirk. "That girl is not frightened one bit."

"Don't be a jerk," I snapped. "Of course she is. She's just making sure no one knows it. Didn't you see her when I mentioned the poltergeist? She practically hit the ceiling."

"Yeah, well, she's ready to go out there and play ball. She didn't collapse or go into hysterics. She is one tough cookie."

"Quit saying that! She's pretending!"

"Well, then, she ought to win an Oscar."

"You just listen to me, David Beanbag-Head DeRemer. I know you think you've won the bet and my cap is practically on your skull, but it isn't. I've got Ash going now, and one more trick should do it. A big one. I mean, a really scary one. And I guarantee it'll get her in trouble with my dad, too. You just wait! Then we'll see who's tough."

David nudged me with the flashlight. "You better watch out, M.J. You might be carrying this too far. You're the one who might wind up in trouble!"

"Now who's being the baby?" I demanded.

But as it turned out, David must have been looking into a crystal ball. Because everything he warned me about came true.

6

The way I had it figured was this.

Ash was teetering on the brink and needed just one more friendly nudge from the resident poltergeist to make her topple and fall. David couldn't see that she was losing her cool. My father and Cory couldn't either. But I could. For some reason, I was beginning to sense the inner workings of my stepsister's mind and I could tell how vulnerable she was. Supergirl had been flying high for too long, and now it was time for a tumble. Embarrassing for her? Sure. A little painful? Maybe. But she deserved to have the wind knocked out of her sails.

It was on Friday, one week before the Phillies game, that I planned the last poltergeist trick. Things had been fairly quiet in the old house. It was time to shake everyone up. Especially Her Iceberg Highness.

My father had announced over lunch that he was finishing up his project. His deadline for mailing the book jacket illustration was Saturday, so he was happy he could wrap it all up one day early. Ash had posed for him the day before, but she had fidgeted too much to give him what he needed. He hadn't understood her mood at the time, but I sure had. The light-bulb explosion had set her back. She may have scoffed at my words in front of David in the basement, but secretly she had believed that the ghost was after her. My next little trick would prove it!

While my father was helping Cory clear the table and do the dishes, and Ash was fiddling around with her hair in the bathroom, I snuck outside. I tiptoed all the way around to the back porch, where I quickly surveyed the scene. My father would usually sit at his worktable with his paints, facing the screened windows. Ash would sit on the small stool directly across from him. Right beside the stool was an old wicker table that held magazines dating back to the prehistoric age and a huge flower vase. Cory liked flowers, and had filled all the rooms with bouquets. She hadn't missed this spot. She had a bunch of colorful roses and daisies massed together in the vase. Hmmm, I thought, perfect. This would just about do it.

I heard my father calling for Ash to quit beautifying herself and come out to the porch in one minute flat. He was ready to start painting. My heart thumping, I tied my trusty thread around a clump of the flower stems. Then I trailed the thread up the screen and out the top part of the window. I dashed out the back door just in time. My father and Ash were coming onto the porch. I ducked down below the windows so they couldn't see me, but I had a firm grasp on the thread that dangled from the screen.

"Is my favorite model ready to strike her infamous pose again?" I heard my father ask and then Ash half groaned, half giggled, and slid onto the stool. From the top of the screen I could see the back of her head. Then to my horror, she swiveled around and I watched her stare into the yard. Another two feet down and she'd spot me, crouching below the window like a Peeping Tom!

I held my breath, closed my eyes, and prayed. She must have continued to stare out the window, because my dad said, "What's so fascinating out there?"

"Nothing," she said slowly, and then hesitated.

"Nothing, but what?"

"Well, you're going to laugh at me, but I get the feeling that someone or some*thing* is watching us."

"Someone or something, like the poltergeist?" My father tried to sound amused, but I detected a sinking note in his voice. Maybe he thought she was looney tunes, too.

"I don't know, Dad. Oh, skip it!"

"Consider it skipped. Now can we get back to work?"

My father walked over to the window, but didn't look out. He arranged Ash's head so that she was facing the flower vase.

Perfectamundo. It couldn't be better if I had set the scene myself. When he moved back to the table, I took hold of the thread and yanked down hard. I could just imagine a whole group of roses and daisies rising as if by magic in the air.

There was silence for a second. Then I heard Ash scream and what sounded like the stool overturning. My father barked, "What in blazes—?" and then gave a muffled curse. Something knocked over, something splashed, and then my father cried out for Cory. Amidst all this ruckus I could hear Ash crying, "I'm sorry! I didn't mean to scare you like that, but the flowers jumped out at me. Oh, I'm sorry, Dad."

There were too many "sorry's" being bandied about. Sorry for what? Something must have happened, but I didn't know what. Then Cory burst onto the porch and gasped.

"Oh, Mark, your painting! It's soaked through! Is it ruined?"

"No, don't touch it!" ordered my father. "You'll only make it worse. No, too late. It's ruined."

"But you were going to mail this off today! What are you going to do?"

There was a long pause. "I don't know," my dad finally said in a strangled voice. "I may wind up losing this job."

"It's my fault!" wailed Ash. "Mine and the poltergeist's! He's the one who did it and ruined your picture. Oh, I hate him. I hate this place. I want to go home!"

And she burst into tears and ran out the screen door—to bump straight into me! We stared at each other and then I hurriedly said: "What's all the noise about? I was coming back from the woods and I could hear you yelling a mile away!"

Ash's bottom lip was trembling. She looked small and lost and about six years old. I felt rotten and guilty and eleven years old—going on one hundred.

"The poltergeist!" she said. "Some flowers flew out of

56

the vase and I screamed and fell off the chair and Dad was so surprised he knocked over his water jar and—and, the picture . . ."

She couldn't go on. Through my prank, my father had ruined his artwork and would miss his deadline. And I was to blame. I couldn't even pin this on the poltergeist.

I had really messed up, as in capital *M*, capital *U*. I would really be in big trouble if anyone found out the truth.

Later on, when everything had quieted down, I snuck back to the porch. I had to remove the damaging evidence that circled the flowers. But the "guilty" roses and daisies had been thrown away and I couldn't find the thread anywhere!

By Saturday morning, I was a basket case.

Any minute I expected my father to come charging into my room with the thread in his hands, denouncing me as a fraud and a phony and handing me a one-way ticket to Outer Mongolia.

But he never appeared. He was too busy making phone calls to his art director, pleading for an extension on the project, trying to explain the reasons for the delay. Meanwhile everyone tiptoed around and whispered a lot like we were in a funeral parlor. On the Richter Scale of Gloom, the Garrett family was pushing 8.6.

Around one or so, Cory offered to make us something to eat, but Ash said she was going over to visit Charlotte Devlin and would probably have lunch there, and I said I wasn't hungry. How could you think about eating when your father might lose his job and your whole life's ready to go up in smoke?

Just before she left, Ash handed me a note. It was outlined in black Magic Marker and stapled together. It was definitely strange-looking.

"Hey, what's this?"

A long intense look and a finger to her lips. "Read it and see. But don't tell Mom and Dad."

And with that parting shot, the blonde whirlwind was gone. Talk about mystery. What in the world was she up to? I started to rip open the note, when I heard Cory call me to help her with some chores in the kitchen. Grumbling under my breath, I had to postpone reading Ash's mysterious message until we heard steps on the outside porch and then banging on the screen door.

"What next?" Cory muttered. She hurried to the door and barely opened it before David and Berry tumbled inside. They looked as though they had just escaped from the spin cycle of a dryer, all agitated with their hair blown around.

"M.J.! Did you see it? Did you see it?" David raced up to me, his eyes practically bulging, his dark hair a mass of cowlicks. Berry twitched beside him, barely able to contain her excitement.

"What?" I asked. "See what?"

"Ash's invitation! She just gave it to us when she went down the hill."

And David thrust a black-lined note in front of my face—the exact same note I held in my hands.

"Invitation? To what?" Cory said, but I remembered Ash's warning and got my friends outside before she could ask any more questions. David's face nearly turned purple when I refused to talk until we hit the stream, but I didn't want anyone to overhear us.

"Now," I said, stopping and turning, "what's going on? What's all this stuff about an invitation?"

I started to unstaple my note, but Berry grabbed it out of my hands.

"Let me tell you! It's Ash! She's having a séance Sunday night at your house at eight o'clock and we're all invited!"

I stared at her and blinked.

"You heard her," David said.

"I heard her all right, but I—I . . ." I broke off, unable to contain my giggles. "So Miss Hockey Stick U.S.A. isn't made out of wood after all! She's scared, David, and *I'm* the one who scared her."

David frowned. "I don't think it's funny that she's so spooked. And it's not funny about the flower incident, either. She told me about how your father's painting was ruined. You better watch out, M.J., or someone's going to find out it's you playing games all along."

"Yeah, but no one knows yet, David, and no one's ever going to know." I crossed my fingers before continuing. "It's too dangerous to play another trick, not after what happened to my father's painting."

"No more tricks?" David crowed. "No more scaring Ash? That's great, old buddy. Which means everything is calm at your house, Ash doesn't ask to leave, and the baseball cap is mine. Because I win the bet!"

I lowered my voice. "The game's not over yet! The odds are that this séance is going to wind up scaring Ash more than anything else and she's going to pack a suitcase by the end of the night. You wait and see. The tough cookie is going to crumble."

Famous last words.

7

"Now are you sure you two will be all right?" Cory asked for the eighth time. "Mark and I can cancel our plans. We can go to a movie and dancing any time."

It was Sunday night and my father and Cory had decided to go out on the town to celebrate the extension of his deadline. He still wasn't happy about the extra work he had to do, but at least he wouldn't lose this job. We had originally been included in their plans, but Ash quickly put an end to that.

"It's my stomach, I think," she whimpered about seven-thirty. "Maybe something I ate for dinner." And she settled with a droop on the living room sofa. What an actress she was. And what great timing. Because it was too late for my parents to get a sitter and besides, as Ash haughtily informed them, "I'm old enough to be a baby-sitter myself!"

"Oh, I don't know," Cory whispered to my father. "After all that's been going on in this house . . . ?"

My father eyed me, and then Ash, and handed Cory

her purse. "C'mon, B.C. The rug rats will be fine. They'll keep the doors locked and create a mess in the kitchen making ice cream sundaes and try not to kill each other by the time we get home."

"I'd just feel so much better if someone else was with them."

"We'll be fine, Mom, really. We've got the number of the movie theater and you can always call us if you're worried," Ash assured her. "Don't worry."

"You heard the kids," my father said. "Don't worry. Now come on, beautiful, I don't want to miss the beginning of the movie." And laughing, he pulled Cory out the door. She bounced back in to yell, "Lock the door!" and then bounced back out again. Seconds later we heard the car leave the driveway and swing down the road.

On the sofa, Ash jumped up with a giggle and a peek at her watch. "I thought they'd never leave!" she cried. "And it's almost eight. Time for David and Berry to be here."

She flipped back her long hair, caught me staring at her, and then smiled a long, slow, cool smile that had me confused. Why was Ash behaving so peculiarly tonight? Sure, she was "hostessing" a séance and that was peculiar in itself, but you'd think she'd be scared or nervous, not act as though she were throwing a birthday party. All that day and the day before, she had pranced around the place as if she were a cat who had just swallowed a saucerful of cream. There had been an unreadable look in her eyes and sometimes I had caught her watching me the way an alley cat watches a helpless bird. What was she thinking?

What was she up to? Did she really assume she had the power to hold a séance and summon a ghost? Really, it was laughable—I was the Peanut Butter Poltergeist!— and yet somehow I didn't feel like laughing.

Ash dashed off to the kitchen. I started to follow, but the doorbell rang.

"M.J., get it!" she yelled. "But don't let anyone into the kitchen until I say so. Oh, and turn off all the lights."

Yes sir! No sir! I shrugged and did her bidding. After all, I had given her a hard time this past week. When the downstairs was in darkness, I slowly opened the front door and made my Frankenstein's monster face.

"Good evening," I said à la Boris Karloff. "Welcome to Ghoulish Manor."

Berry jumped and then peered uncertainly into the living room.

"It's awful dark in there!" Her voice trembled.

"Hey, now, I warned you," David said beside her. "If you were going to be a scared baby, you couldn't come."

"I'm not!" She tossed her head.

"You better not be. This is all a silly game and nothing's going to happen tonight, so let's just do it to be nice to Ash, but let's get it over with. I promised Pa we'd be home by nine."

I ushered them in and nudged David. "With what Ashley has in store, I'm sure you'll be back by eight-thirty."

He grinned but said, "We'll see."

We waited in the darkened living room, listening to the sound of the crickets and the occasional croak of a bullfrog in the nearby stream. Once in a while, a car would pass the house, its headlights casting shadows in the room. The stillness and the blackness were getting to me.

"Ash!" I shouted. "It's after eight!"

Silence.

"Ash?"

More silence. Just as I got up, however, the kitchen door opened and Ash appeared holding a lit candle. She didn't say a word, just stood there and let the candlelight make hollows in her face.

"Well, what's the big idea?" I blustered. "Are you inviting us in for this séance or not?"

Without losing her blank expression, she held out her hand and beckoned to us, then moved silently back into the kitchen.

"I don't like this," Berry whispered. "Ash is acting funny."

"Well, that's nothing new," I said. "Besides, we told you the séance would be funny."

We all moved together to the door. David went in first, followed by Berry, while I hesitated outside for a second.

Step into my parlor, said the spider to the fly.

I made a face and then took the plunge.

"Ready or not," I said, laughing. "Here I come!"

"You've got to take this seriously, M.J., or it won't work!"

Ash's voice was low and intense. And very disapproving.

Geez, who did she think she was, one of my teachers?

I skidded to a stop and raised my hand as if taking a vow: "I solemnly swear I will take all this séance stuff—

er—business extra ultraseriously and will not giggle, laugh, or make a fool of myself once during the next hour. If I do so, I will let myself be strung up by my thumbs, and my honored baseball cards and favorite comic books may be given away. Amen." I looked across at Ash. "That serious enough for you?"

She stood at the kitchen table, still holding the candle aloft, a ghostbusting Statue of Liberty. David and Berry had taken their places around the table, and now everyone was waiting for me to do likewise. The Python Princess sniffed for effect and put the candle in the middle of the table. She pointed to my seat, one facing the screened porch, and I sat down.

Under the table, to my right, David gave me a kick, and I stifled a yelp. I rubbed my knee, and he leaned over to whisper in perfect Ash imitation: "You've got to take this seriously."

We bent our heads together and fought back laughter, but the situation worsened when Berry piped up, "What are you two talking about?"

"Nothing." David's voice quavered and he avoided my eyes. "Nothing at all."

"That's good," Ash cut in, "because I'm ready to begin. And I need your total, absolute attention." Those *Children of the Damned* eyes stared at each one of us in turn until we subsided like meek little lambs. "Good. The first thing we do is clear our minds and try to think only of the Peanut Butter Poltergeist. All right, everyone close your eyes and think about the poltergeist."

I glanced over at David with a smirk and we bit our lips.

"Close your eyes, I said!"

"Yes, ma'am!" I gave a sharp salute, then obeyed orders.

We sat like silent mummies for what seemed like hours, and I started to fidget. Come on, Ashley, I wanted to say. Do your stuff, shriek, wail, or thump on the table, but get *something* going. This eye-closing stuff was putting everyone to sleep.

And then a cool gust of air seemed to slide along my neck, and I shivered. As if Ash could read my mind. But that was nonsense. And then she said, "All right, open them," and clapped her hands. We all blinked and grinned foolishly at one another in the candlelight.

The grins faded, however, at the sight that greeted us on the table.

"What's that?" Berry asked.

"A Ouija board," I replied and then groaned. How hokey could my stepsister get? Ouija boards were for little kids or quacks or all-girl slumber parties. This séance had plunged to a new low. Ash must have sensed my disdain because her face seemed to flush.

"All right," she said, "everybody put your fingers on the planchette."

My, my. Wasn't she getting technical. Using the big term for that tiny plastic triangle. I rolled my eyes, but obeyed orders.

David and Berry squeezed their fingers on the Ouija

pointer, and Ash slid hers on, too. We were all jammed up.

"Not too much room," I complained.

"Never mind, keep your thumbs off and close your eyes. All right, silence."

Once again, we listened to one another breathe and then Ash cleared her throat. "We are trying to make contact with the Peanut Butter Poltergeist. Is he out there tonight?"

Silence. Heavy breathing. Berry's in anticipation, mine in disgust.

"I repeat, we are trying to make contact with the Peanut Butter Poltergeist. Is he here with us now?"

Was it my imagination or did the plastic pointer quiver? Yes. It quivered and trembled, then slid as if under its own steam to the *Yes* printed on the board.

We all opened our eyes.

"Yes!" Berry cried. "He's here!"

"Ho, boy," I muttered. "And so's Santa Claus. And so's—"

"Silence!" Ash barked. She glared at me. "Disbelief will scare him away. Now, let's continue. Poltergeist, or spirit, if you're here, who do you want to speak to?"

Again, our fingers trembled on the pointer, and after a long pause, it moved very slowly, very deliberately over to the alphabet part of the board, where it came to rest at *M*.

"*M*," David said, poking me under the table with his foot.

The pointer quivered, then swung back until it stopped at *J*.

69

"*J!*" David cried. "M.J.!"

"Oh, sure," I snorted. "You guys all pushed it."

"I didn't," David swore. "Honest!"

"Me neither!" Berry cried.

"Don't look at me," Ash said coolly. "The spirit talks through the board. We don't control it. It controls us."

"Well, that's just super. So the poltergeist is right here in this room and he wants to talk to me. Well, go ahead, Poltergeist. Do your thing. I'm all yours."

I leaned back with a chuckle, and that's when the heavy pounding started.

"Wha-what's that?" David said. He looked at me and gulped. "Quit doing that, M.J.!"

"Doing what, for pete's sake! I'm sitting right here! And it sounds like it's coming from under our feet!"

We looked under the table. Nothing. The pounding stopped.

"I don't get it," I said and looked at Ash. But her eyes showed as much confusion as everyone else's. "Aren't you faking this for the séance?"

"No!"

"No?"

"Oh, Poltergeist," she cried, throwing open her arms, "if you're here, show us. Show us—now!"

We sat upright in our seats, me slightly puzzled, but sure it was a game, when the kitchen door creaked. Then a strong gust of cold air blew it open with a crash and, while Berry shrieked, the candle went out. Something heavy rolled into the room and landed right by my feet.

70

"What in the . . . ?" I fumbled around and picked up the object. Even in the dark I could tell what it was: the peanut butter jar. The hair on the back of my head suddenly stood on end, even though I knew it was a game. *Hoped* it was a game. *Prayed* it was.

"What is it, M.J.?" David asked. He sounded scared.

I croaked out a laugh. "The peanut butter jar."

I passed it around the table, while Ash kept inviting the poltergeist to appear. But right at that minute, in the dark, I just wanted her to stop. Too many odd things were happening and I didn't like it.

And then, David clutched my arm so tight that I yelled. "Hey, quit it! What's gotten into you?"

He couldn't get a word out, just jumped up and pointed in the direction of the porch. I stared and what I saw there I will never forget, not when I'm forty and fading, not when I'm a professional ball player for a team like the Phillies. The image will always remain locked in my mind.

First we saw a light, kind of dim, kind of yellow. Maybe a candle, maybe a flashlight. It was glowing in the darkness of our backyard. Then we saw that the light was moving, coming closer to the house. The closer it got, the more my knees shook. I tried to stop them, but I couldn't. Then my teeth started chattering and my heart began pounding. I tried to speak, to come out with a funny remark, but I couldn't. My lips were wobbling as hard as my knees.

Ash seemed hypnotized by the sight. She leaned over to me and whispered, "It's coming to you, M.J.!"

71

Not if I could help it. But my legs wouldn't obey my brain. So I just had to sit there, helpless, while David held on to my arm. He was as frightened as I was.

The "thing" got worse. Whatever was carrying the light was shrouded in black, invisible. But when the light got close to the outside screen window, some kind of hood was thrown back and this horrible, glowing ghoul face stared in at us. Smiled at us, the candle or flashlight intensifying the awful craters of its face, the eyes red sockets, the lips all melted looking. It looked around the room, then stopped when its eyes rested on me! I could feel the intensity of its gaze.

"M.J.!" Ash breathed. "Talk to it! Ask it what it wants so it'll go away and leave our family alone!"

Who could talk? Who could think?

When the "thing" reached out a hand—or claw, whatever it had—to rap on the locked porch door, David and I both let out bloodcurdling screams, amplified in stereo. Berry jumped up, I jumped up, David jumped up, and we all ran out of the room—leaving Ash crying, "There now, you've scared it, M.J.! It's disappeared. Oh, M.J., how could you?"

8

I slept with the light on that night.

Call me a baby. Call me a chicken. I had seen what I had seen and no way was I staying in the dark for more than a second.

The next morning I decided to do some exploring. While everyone was busy fixing pancakes and bacon in the kitchen, I tiptoed around to the backyard. What was I looking for? Who knows! Some piece of evidence that told me the ghost had been real. But ghosts don't leave candle holders or flashlight batteries behind. And ghosts don't leave footprints, either. I pored over the ground, my nose so close to the grass I could hear the ants singing, but found nothing.

"M.J., what on earth are you looking for out there?" my father called from the porch. "Didn't you hear us? Breakfast is ready."

"I'll be right there, Dad."

"Do you need any help? Did you lose something?"

Just my marbles, I wanted to say. And yeah, Dad, thanks a lot, Dad, you can help. I'm looking for the calling card of the Peanut Butter Poltergeist. Oh, didn't you know, Dad? He paid us a friendly little visit last night. And he seemed to want to talk to me.

I stood up in the warm summer sunshine and shivered. How was I going to get through the next six days?

Right after breakfast, I decided I needed to talk to somebody before I went crazy. And it couldn't be Ash. She wasn't any help.

"Where are you headed?" she asked when I came barreling downstairs and headed for the front door.

"I'm going to town."

"To see David?"

I wasn't sure. Town meant the DeRemer family, but it also meant the small sheriff's office and it also meant the local library. At this point, I didn't know if I needed to blurt my fears out to my friend, the police, or the librarian. I needed a sturdy dose of courage, but I also needed protection and information. I didn't know where to turn or what to do first. The two people I wanted to talk to but couldn't were Cory and my father. Ash had sworn us to secrecy regarding the poltergeist. I couldn't break a promise. Also, how would it look if I confessed that I had been the poltergeist from the very beginning? They wouldn't like it. Not in a million years.

The only person I could talk to was David. He'd understand my fears. Ashley only scoffed at them. She seemed to think unearthing the spirit of the poltergeist was the greatest thing to hit the light since King Tut. If I had any doubts before about how tough she was, I didn't now. The Python Princess had been the only one to stand her ground when the monster appeared. She was unreal, my stepsister.

Now I looked at her with renewed resentment.

"What are all the questions, the third degree? I'm just going out."

"Touchy, touchy. What's bugging you?"

"As if you didn't know," I hissed. "You and your stupid idea, holding the séance. Bringing the ghost out from hiding. It was fine before you went and did that."

"Really? You think so? All the damage he was doing to our house and ruining Dad's painting was fine?"

"Well, no, but . . ."

Just then, Cory came walking down the steps with a jar of peanut butter in her hands and an annoyed look on her face.

"M.J., please don't leave food in your room like that. You know how I feel about messes."

My jaw dropped. "What mess? And I didn't put that peanut butter jar in my room. I never touched it."

"Well, I found it right outside your door, and also peanut butter smears on the walls. Now I hope this doesn't happen again. All we need in this house are ants or bugs. Ugh!" And with a grimace, she walked into the kitchen.

"But I—I didn't do it!"

Ash looked at me with rounded eyes. "You mean it?"

"Yes."

"He's back," she whispered, clapping her hands in delight. "He's come back and he's found your room! Oh,

M.J., this is so exciting! Now you have the chance of making contact with him and asking him to leave us alone. I know that's what he wants."

Well, it sure ain't what I wanted. I made a beeline for the door.

Someone had to help me, and help me fast. Otherwise I'd have a ghostly encounter of the peanut butter kind. And it was going to turn out more than a little sticky.

It was David who hit upon the brilliant scheme.

This Einstein was not thinking too straight.

"We're going to exorcise the ghost," he announced, pounding a fist into the palm of his hand. "It's as simple as that."

"What do we look up in the yellow pages, *E* for exorcising or *G* for ghostbusting?"

"Very funny, but it's not that complicated. There's one person who can help us and I know where to reach her. Come on!"

He scrambled to his feet and I followed him. I'd follow my friend anywhere if he could eliminate this spirit from my life.

"Where we going?"

"About one hundred feet, into the coffee shop. This person eats at my dad's place every Monday, Wednesday, and Friday without fail."

Mrs. Harrower was sitting at the counter polishing off a BLT when we raced into the shop. She was wearing a dark, professional business suit and had her silvery hair swept up away from her face, but her bright dangling earrings stood out, and in the heat, her little bow tie had wilted. She looked grandmotherly and conservative, and about as far from a ghostbuster as I'd ever imagined.

"This isn't going to work," I said peevishly. "No way. This sweet little old lady combating the gruesome ghoul? I don't see it."

"Look at it this way," David retorted. "What other choice have you got?"

Wise words.

We waved hello to Kathy and Donna, the waitresses, and approached Mrs. Harrower. She sat there, blithely munching on her sandwich, little knowing the supernatural challenge that awaited her.

"You talk to her," I whispered to David. "I can't."

"Baby."

You got that right. "Go ahead!"

He cleared his throat and tapped Mrs. Harrower on the shoulder.

"Why, Davey and Mikey, I mean, M.J.! Coming here for lunch today?"

Her good-natured face beamed at us, and I almost cut and run. But David gripped my arm.

"Mrs. Harrower, could we come talk to you about a problem we're having? Well, that M.J.'s having?" He lowered his voice. "It's about the strange things that have been going on at his family's place. They've taken, well, a turn for the worse. And M.J.'s involved up to his eyeballs."

Batty Dotty's eyes had flickered at the mention of strange things, and now she was practically shredding the remains of her BLT in her excitement.

"Tell me," she breathed. "I must hear all."

David proceeded to give her the edited version of the séance and then of the peanut butter jar incident that morning. He neglected to mention that fact that I had been the poltergeist the week before. We didn't want anything to sway Mrs. Harrower in the wrong direction.

But Mrs. Harrower accepted David's story without the blink of an eye or a skeptical look. That's what was so great about Batty Dotty. She didn't behave like an adult at all! She took us seriously. She took us so seriously she wanted to have a little session as soon as possible.

"I must get to the bottom of this," she murmured, wrenching open her handbag to produce a small black datebook. She thumbed through it rapidly. "Let's see, what do my appointments look like? I've got to show a house at one o'clock, another at three, then a meeting back at the office. I won't be free until five or so. Can you make it then, at my place?"

I looked across at David and calculated rapidly. Cory liked to have dinner at six or so. Maybe I could persuade her to hold it for me if I said I'd be helping David at his father's boat place. I'd give it a try.

David looked at me and nodded. He'd be there, too. He'd arrange something with his father. We both knew where the local witch lived and weren't all that crazy keen to visit her place, but I'd go through the most terrifying fun house around to get the poltergeist out of my hair.

9

~~~~~~~~~~

I arrived at Mrs. Harrower's house a few minutes before five that evening. The town witch lived in a heavily wooded section, almost creepy in its absolute stillness. As I walked up the gravel path, a small creature—a squirrel or bird—rustled in the nearby bushes. At least I *hoped* it was an animal, and not the poltergeist. I muttered under my breath and jogged the remaining way to the cottage, hoping David would be waiting outside for me.

He wasn't. I had to walk up to Mrs. Harrower's door alone, and what I saw nailed there didn't reassure me. A grotesque-looking mask with slits for eyes and a beaked nose leered at me.

"Take me to your leader," I said, raising a hand in salutation.

The face frowned back at me, silent as the tomb and almost as scary.

"Come on, David," I prayed, glancing nervously over my shoulder. "Hurry up. I need you for moral support tonight!"

I started counting to a hundred and paced. No way was I entering the witch's lair alone. Mrs. Harrower was a white or good witch, as she often said, but she was still a witch. That meant she dabbled in things unknown. And I had had my fill recently of just such things.

When I had counted to sixty-seven, I heard footsteps behind me. I turned around with a grateful smile but it faded somewhat when I saw Berry tagging alongside her brother. And David had a scowl on his face.

"What's going on?"

"I'm baby-sitting tonight, believe it or not. Of all the lousy luck! Pa had an emergency with one of the rental boats. It sprung a leak near Fred Willert's dock. So guess who gets to watch monkeyface here?"

She aimed a kick at his shin. "Don't call me that!"

Brother and sister tussled for a while until the door opened and Mrs. Harrower peered out at us. What a strange sight we must have been—recess time at kindergarten. But she held out both arms in welcome.

"Greetings, greetings, my friends. Won't you please grace my humble portal with your presence."

"Presents?" said David under his breath. "We didn't bring any presents. Were we supposed to?"

Mrs. Harrower let out a booming stage laugh. *"Mon enfant,"* she cried, *"quel charmant.* No, no, no cause for alarm. My services are free. The only payment I seek is your happiness and peace of mind."

Amen to that, Sister Dorothea! She ushered us into the small hall and then pointed to the living room. All the curtains had been drawn and there were no lights on, just

80

the glow of fat black candles. But we could still make out all the old-fashioned broomsticks fastened to the staircase. I was wondering how many miles she got to the gallon, when she said, "Please, sit down."

The three of us looked around uncertainly. There was so much clutter in the small room, so many pieces of furniture and bric-a-brac that we didn't know where to sit. Sure, there were chairs, a sofa, and even a rocking chair, but knitting and newspapers and cats covered each seat. I'm not talking kitty cats here, but Incredible Hulk feline creatures. There were scores of them, in all shapes and colors, clinging to the seats of the chairs.

Mrs. Harrower saw our confusion and took pity on us. With a few windmill-like motions and cries of *Shoo!*, she cleared off a portion of the sofa. We squeezed in together and Mrs. Harrower took the rocking chair across from us.

"Now then," she said brightly, "where should we start?"

I looked at David, he looked at me, Berry kept her eyes glued to Mrs. Harrower.

"I think," I began hesitantly, "that you should call the spirit and then squash it dead before it makes any more trouble."

"My dear young man, the spirit is already quite dead. And although I boast some other-dimensional, unusual powers, they are not used to harm or hurt, but to help, in a positive way."

"Well, then, can't you positively help the monster out of town, and do it as fast as you can before he does me in?"

81

"He's not out to harm you, M.J.," Mrs. Harrower assured me. "Studies show that poltergeists have never physically injured human beings. They're just playful little spirits who have somehow gotten hooked into the tensions of a young person."

"This poltergeist is not little," I said. "And he doesn't look playful to me."

"He's an ugly monster," David agreed and Berry nodded.

"Now, now," the good witch said, "beauty is in the eye of the beholder. I think what we should do is have me get a feel for this being and what he wants. Did you bring me anything he's actually touched or used?"

My face fell. "I don't know of anything he's actually touched, except—wait a second! The peanut butter jar! He seems to lurk around that a lot. But I can't go home and get it, there'd be too many questions."

"Never mind. I'll use my trusty crystal. That should do it."

She got up and went to the fireplace mantel, where she extracted something from a small box. It was a small, sparkling, clear ball, set on a long gold chain. I breathed a sigh of relief. If she had returned with a crystal *ball*, I would have walked out. I mean, how corny can you get? As if sensing my thoughts, she smiled.

"This little object has produced some wonderful results. It need not take much to tap into the 'other world.' Now then, let us be completely silent, as silent as snow, as silent as the night, so that I may commune with the spirit."

Mrs. Harrower sat down, then gazed intently into the crystal. Every so often, she'd set the ball rocking and her eyes would follow the motion. She sat like that for a long time, and the three of us fidgeted on the sofa. What was worse, the hypnotic motion of the swaying crystal was slowly putting Berry to sleep and making me seasick.

Suddenly, Mrs. Harrower let out a long sigh and settled back against the rocker with closed eyes.

"Hey!" David poked me. "Is she going to sleep?"

"Shh. She's in a trance, I think." I didn't know, but I hoped that's what it was. Batty Dotty's lips twitched and her fingers rolled the crystal around and around.

Mrs. Harrower came to with a start. She blinked at us in a fuzzy way, and when she spoke, her voice was hushed so we had to strain to hear.

"I've made communication of a sort with your friend, M.J. He definitely feels something for you. Something that you may have done last week . . . ?"

David practically punched me in the ribs, he was so excited. I felt myself get hot and prayed my guilty face wouldn't give me away. Had I really made the poltergeist materialize with my crazy scheme? Was I the one he gravitated toward?

I shook my head and mumbled something.

"Don't look like it's the end of the world, child. I learned something about him that might make him rest easy. It's something you have to do because he's focused on you."

"What? I'll do anything!" Except face him, of course. Oh, please don't ask me to do that.

"Here's what it is. To get his spirit to rest, you must lead him out to Black Lake and hurl him into the water. His spirit belongs there, he needs to go back."

I jumped off the sofa. "But I can't do that! He's huge, that thing. And what makes you think he'll follow me out to the lake?"

"I bet Ash could do it," Berry piped up. "She's not afraid of the poltergeist at all."

"Yeah," Benedict Arnold David agreed. "Couldn't Ash do it for M.J.?"

Mrs. Harrower shook her head. "I'm sorry, but it's something only M.J. can do. M.J., are you up to it?"

I gazed at her dumbly. My reputation was at stake. I was a quivering mess, but I had to say yes. To prove I was as brave as Ash. To keep the monster away from my family.

I looked across at Mrs. Harrower and slowly nodded my head.

She beamed proudly back at me. "All right, young man. Then listen carefully. Here are your instructions."

Hurry! Hurry! Hurry! Reserve your seats now for the monsterweight fight of the century: Nerdlebrain Michael Joseph takes on the Peanut Butter Poltergeist. Wednesday at twelve midnight. Location of match: the dock at Black Lake.

I could afford to be brave about my "date" with the ghostman—even joke about it—because Mrs. Harrower told me I didn't have to confront him face-to-face. I had

85

been instructed to take the peanut butter jar and march that to the lake and throw it in. That was a whole lot better for my health than escorting the spirit in ghoulish person! And since Mrs. Harrower seemed to believe the poltergeist wanted that, I thought I was getting off with a light sentence. After Wednesday night, the Garrett family could rest easy, and I would live to see the ripe old age of twelve.

But whether my stepsister would make it to thirteen was another matter altogether.

In the two days since my visit to Mrs. Harrower, Ash had been acting pretty obnoxiously, and I was tempted to dump her in the lake instead of the jar. I don't know what was making her behave that way, but she strutted around, boasting of her bravery at the séance and then yelling at me for scaring the poltergeist away.

"If you hadn't screamed like a baby," she said in a disgusted voice, "we might have been able to communicate with the thing." And she glared at me.

"Well, ex-c-u-u-u-se me." I glared back. "Tell it to drop me a line and get the zip code right if he wants to communicate with me so badly. Or better yet, have it call me person to person. I'm not going anywhere."

"My, my, aren't we the tough guy! What happened to the scared little kid of Sunday night?"

"What scared little kid?" I scoffed. Sure, I could act tough now because I assumed the worst was over. I hadn't seen one particle of the poltergeist since he put the peanut butter jar in my room, and I hoped he'd remain invisible.

And once I put him to bed tonight in the lake, I assumed he'd stay there. He'd be happy where he belonged, according to Mrs. Harrower, and so would I. Brother, so would I!

The Python Princess narrowed her eyes and slithered closer. "Don't be so sure of yourself," she whispered. "The ghost is still around. And he wants you. I can feel it." And with a flounce, she walked away.

I had to laugh. Ash was trying to scare me, but it wouldn't work. She didn't know about my visit to Mrs. Harrower, and I wasn't about to tell her. Both David and Berry were impressed by my decision to tackle the Peanut Butter Poltergeist, and I didn't want Ash spoiling it for me. Knowing her, she'd demand to come along and I didn't want her stealing my thunder. No, the job tonight was mine and mine alone. But after her warning, I wasn't so sure of myself. Was the ghost still around, waiting to get me alone in the dark? Would he really go peacefully into the lake or would he *poof! bam!* materialize out of the peanut butter jar and bend my all-too-human and all-too-puny body out of shape?

I shook my head. I didn't want to think about it. Geez, that Ash was loathsome!

At a quarter to twelve that night, I was ready. I was scared, I hated to admit it, but I was ready—the baseball cap defiantly stuck on my head, my trusty flashlight in one hand and the peanut butter jar in the other. I tiptoed down the steps, being extra careful to avoid creaking so Ash wouldn't wake up. I pulled open the front door and hesitated. The trees were swaying and bending under the winds of an approaching storm, leaves whispering eerily together.

"Don't go out," they seemed to moan. "Danger."

Heavy black clouds rolled across the sky, obliterating the moon. I took a tentative step outside and felt a plop of rain.

"Oh, great," I muttered. "This is terrific. A perfect night for skinny-dipping with ghosts and walking alone in the woods. All I need now is thunder and lightning and—"

A jagged flash of light cut me off, and I heard the crash of thunder a few seconds later.

"That does it," I whispered angrily to hide my fear. "Time to get this show on the road." I glanced down at the peanut butter jar. "And you be a good boy and stay in there. You'll be home at the bottom of the lake before you know it."

I took a deep breath and made a run for the woods. The light drizzle was threatening to turn into a downpour, but I wasn't about to go back and get my umbrella. How sissy can you get? The ground was getting muddy, and my running shoes were soaked, but I plowed on ahead. I had to toss the jar into the lake at twelve midnight on the button. And, checking my watch, I saw that time was running out. Once I hit the woods, I turned on the flashlight, but I didn't want to see what was hiding in the dark. It was bad enough the wind was howling and the leaves were rustling and the thunder and lightning were providing the spooky sound effects and light show. If I ever get

back alive, I vowed, I will never go see another horror movie again!

I crawled under low branches, water dripping down my neck, and came upon Black Lake in the clearing. There was the dock, glistening in the rain, and I stopped beneath a big oak tree to catch my breath.

Okay, okay, okay, I chanted to myself. This is it. The moment you've been waiting for. I rested the flashlight on the ground, and held the jar in my trembling hands.

"Time to go beddy-bye," I whispered and then felt something grip my shoulders from behind.

10

I wheeled around and let out a gasp.

There stood David, drenched to the skin, sheepishly grinning at me. I took a step toward him and he held out his hand.

"Hey, take it easy! I'm your friend, not your enemy, remember? I figured you'd need some moral support on a night like this."

"Moral support, yes, but not heart failure. Geez, David, you really scared me."

For some reason I found myself whispering, and David was too. I guess that showed how much we believed that *something* was out there listening.

As if on cue, I heard a rustling sound deep in the bushes. I nudged David and pointed and he made a face.

"It's just an animal, probably."

And then I heard what sounded like a low moan and the back of my neck prickled. I looked at David. He looked at me, then punched my arm.

"Forget about that! It's nearly twelve. You've got to throw the jar in the lake at twelve on the dot."

"I got so spooked I almost forgot! No, don't come with me. I've got to do this alone."

Big words, little man. I smiled, but my heart was thumping and my palms were sweating. A lot of "what if's" danced through my mind. *What if* the poltergeist came out of the jar as I was about to throw it in the water? *What if* Mrs. Harrower guessed wrong and he didn't want to take a swim at all? Forget it. It was too late to back out now. I had come this far. I had to finish the job.

I left David under the safe umbrella of the oak and edged forward. Right, left. Right, left. My feet were moving awfully slowly.

From behind me David hissed, "Get going! It's nearly twelve!"

The dock loomed up. I took a deep breath and stepped on it. Did the jar quiver in my hands? Or was that the product of my imagination? Go on, M.J., I urged myself. Only six more feet to go. I walked to the very edge of the dock with my eyes half-closed and my breath coming in ragged gasps in my throat.

"Peanut Butter Poltergeist," I whispered, holding up the jar, "don't pull any funny stuff on me now."

I counted aloud, "one, two" but when I reached "three," a huge shape loomed up from beneath the dock and grabbed hold of my arm.

I staggered back and David shrieked, "Run, M.J., run! It's the ghost! Let's get out of here!" And I heard him go crashing through the woods as if the poltergeist were hot on his trail. I wanted to run, too, but couldn't. The dark shape grappled with me so I couldn't escape. Suddenly, the thing wobbled and letting go with a gasp, lost its balance and toppled into the lake! I realized with a start that it had been standing up in a canoe, half-hidden beneath the end of the dock. So much for supernatural materializations. A light flickered at the back of my mind, but it wasn't until I kneeled down to get a closer look at the dark shape that I put two and two together.

I saw a hand beat at the water, then a black hood fall away and silvery blonde hair fan out. I heard a gravel pit voice sputter, and I cried: "Ash! Is that you?"

"Help!" she cried. "I'm drowning!"

I leaned over the edge and offered her my outstretched hand. "You can't. It's not that deep. Just grab hold of my hand and stand up."

She couldn't reach me, just floundered around, screeching. I rolled my eyes. Geez, women. And then it hit me. This was the Python Princess making all this racket. Ms. Tough Guy herself dissolving into baby wails. It would serve her right if I just walked away and left her. I mean, after what she had just pulled, practically aging me overnight!

But she was thrashing about so helplessly and making such a fuss, that I took a deep breath and jumped into the lake. The muddy bottom sucked at my feet, but the water reached only to my chest. I was okay. I grabbed hold of Ash's arms and began pulling her, pushing her out of the water. She put up quite a squawking but finally staggered out with me onto dry land, where she immediately began sniffling.

I looked at her with mingled disbelief and irritation.

"Want to tell me what this game was all about tonight?"

She was wearing a navy hooded sweatshirt and dark jeans and was crumpled into a soggy ball on the ground. She looked about as tough as one of her stuffed toys. Now she peered up at me through dripping hair.

"It was to get back at you," she said in between shivers, "for pretending to be the Peanut Butter Poltergeist last week and making the vase crash in my room and scaring me."

I choked, but covered it with a laugh. "That's crazy."

"I know all about your little midnight games, M.J., and I know about the light bulb and the flowers and the alarm clock and the paintings crashing. Oh, and I also know about your bet with David, trying to scare me so you could go to your stupid baseball game. That was really lamebrain."

"Was it as lamebrain as you coming out here and waiting for me in a canoe? Hey! Wait a second! How did you find out about the plan tonight?"

"Berry told me. She told me everything that happened at Mrs. Harrower's place, too."

"That little rat!"

"She's no more of a rat than you and David are, lying to everybody and sneaking around. Pretending there was a poltergeist when there really wasn't."

I looked down at her. "How can you say that? You're the one who threw the séance and conjured up the poltergeist. You saw him! We all did!"

A giggle escaped her. "I have to admit, she was pretty scary."

"She?"

"Yes, Charlotte Devlin. She was the poltergeist. I let her into the house Sunday night when you were all waiting in the living room and put her in the cellar. She pounded on the walls, then she came back upstairs through the side door and went around to roll the peanut butter jar into the kitchen. But the best part was her mask. Boy, that was real. And oh Lord, if you could have seen your face! What a riot! It was worth all the effort and planning just to see the look on your face."

And she burst out laughing. I scowled and kicked at the ground. I had been taken! I had been tricked, and by the worst person possible, my stepsister. I had to wipe the smug grin off her face.

"Wait until I tell Dad and Cory about what you did."

"Go ahead. You tell them, and I'll tell them about your being the poltergeist. And I have proof that you pulled the flowers out of the vase and wrecked Dad's project. I found the string."

She had me. It was a standoff.

I looked down at the peanut butter jar. "So there was nothing really to this? This is just a plain old jar of peanut butter with no ghost or spirit in it?"

"I'm afraid so." She got up slowly and shook herself all over like a dog, splattering water everywhere.

I tightened my lips and picked up the jar. Then I stretched back my arm and hurled it as hard and as far as I could into the lake. It made a nice and heavy sound as it hit the surface and then sank.

"Bye-bye, poltergeist," I said bitterly.

Ash shivered beside me. "Come on, let's go home. I'm getting soaked out here in the rain."

I turned and walked away from her.

"Hey!" she cried. "Wait up!"

I just walked faster. This story was not going to have a happy ending. I was not going to get to the Phillies game after all, I was going to lose my baseball cap to David, and more than that, I was going to look like a fool when the story of what actually happened at the dock came out.

There might not be a poltergeist in Langtown, but there was certainly a curse on me.

"Michael Joseph, Ashley Avis, get in here," said my father in the grimmest voice I had ever heard him use. "You two have some explaining to do."

He and Cory huddled together on the front porch, watching Ash and me straggle up the path.

"Just great," I muttered under my breath. I could see the headlines now: SUMMER BOY LAUGHINGSTOCK OF LANGTOWN! and M.J. GARRETT GROUNDED FOR FIFTEEN YEARS! A confrontation with my parents was the last thing I expected. All I wanted to do was come home and dry off and then go to sleep for maybe a hundred years or at least until the shame wore off.

It was not to be.

Especially when I saw why. As Ash and I walked into the house—the condemned prisoners marching to the gallows—David jumped up from the sofa.

"M.J.! You're alive! You're all right!" He gaped at me, then at Ash. "Ash! Where did you come from? How did you guys escape from the"—he lowered his voice when my parents entered the room—"monster!"

I couldn't speak. I'd be ruined if I did. David had tried to be a friend and save my skin by getting help from my parents, but it had been the wrong move. I glanced at Ash, but she had her jaw stuck out in front of her and wouldn't look at me. My heart sank. She was angry. It would all come out now. Every stupid prank I had pulled.

My father towered over me. "All right, M.J. Would you please tell me what you were doing down at the dock at twelve o'clock at night? In this weather? And why David here kept telling us to get the police to save you from a fate worse than death? Cory and I have been out of our minds with worry."

"And what were you doing there, too, Ashley?" Cory burst out. My stepmother's usually neat hair was uncombed and her eyes looked red. She was a wreck.

Silence prevailed in the room. There was only the sound of the rain drumming on the roof and an occasional burst of thunder.

I looked down at my soaked pants and shoes, a muddy mess, and thought rapidly.

"M.J., I'm waiting," my father said very slowly.

"Ashley Avis, *I'm* waiting," Cory repeated.

And although he didn't say it, David was waiting, too. All beside himself to hear how his good friend escaped the clutches of the poltergeist.

I let out a resigned sigh. Time to take the medicine, but oh brother, how bitter it would taste.

"Aw, you're not gonna believe it," I began, "but I went to Black Lake tonight to—well, to . . ." I stopped, getting up the courage to take the plunge, when Ash smoothly cut in, "To look for night crawlers. We both did."

My father took a step back. "Night crawlers?"

David took a step forward. "Night crawlers!"

Cory didn't move anywhere, just mouthed, "Night crawlers?" Then she shook her head. "What in goodness' name are night crawlers?"

"Bait," my dad said blankly. "For fishing. But why in heaven's name were you digging around for them at this ridiculous hour? And look at your clothes. And your hair. The both of you. You look like the night crawlers were digging around for you."

He directed the question at me, but I waited for Ash to answer. She had done the impossible and pulled the rabbit out of the hat the first time. Maybe she'd do it on the second.

"Well—ah—" she stammered, "um—Charlotte Devlin's brother told us the best time to catch night crawlers was at night during a rainstorm and M.J. wanted to take me fishing one last time before we left, so we needed bait fast, and well"—she threw up her hands and beamed cherubically—"we didn't think it would be dangerous to go out for just a short while tonight."

"You didn't think, period," Cory snapped. "Of all the unthinking, foolish things to do. And you still didn't explain why you're both so filthy dirty and drenched. Not to mention why David was telling us you were in some kind of grave danger."

I directed a daggers look at David, who seemed to shrink four inches.

"I don't know," I mumbled. "Nothing really happened."

My father's eyes were steely. "No dice. I don't believe you. Now for the last time, what really happened at Black Lake? And if you don't tell me now, you're going to be in some mighty serious trouble."

"Don't blame M.J.," Ash suddenly cried. "It's all my fault. See, I was running around on the dock, trying to be funny, and I tripped and fell in the water. Maybe that's what David saw, only he didn't realize it was me."

Cory's eyes practically bulged. "You fell in the lake? You could have drowned! You know you can't swim!"

"But I didn't, Mom. Because M.J. saved me. He jumped in and pulled me to shore."

My stepmother's lips started trembling, and with a fierce motion she pulled Ash to her. "My baby," she cried, hugging her. "Oh, my poor baby."

Ash was off the hook. She peeked over her mother's arms and winked at me. I looked at her for a few confusing moments, and then I winked back. Earth finally making contact with the space creature. It was a strange, yet oddly natural feeling.

100

My father cleared his throat. "Is that true, son?" he asked gruffly. Ninety percent of it was, so I nodded.

"All right, then," he continued, shaking his head. "I don't like what you kids did, going off alone so late like that, and on such a lousy night, but I guess I have a few tales to tell of when I was your age. And I'm proud of you for coming to your stepsister's rescue. We all are."

"Come here, M.J.," Cory said, holding her arms out. I went into them for the biggest hug she'd ever given me. "Thank you, son."

I smiled shyly up at her. "That's okay . . . Mom."

And she squeaked with pleasure and nearly broke my ribs.

I couldn't believe how it all turned out. My fatal foe and archrival had stuck up for me. We had emerged victorious from a disastrous night—together. Two sworn enemies had become the Odd Couple.

Suddenly my parents remembered the time and told David they'd drive him home. When my father was warming up the car and my stepmother was fishing out boots and umbrellas, David raced up to me.

"Look," he whispered, "I saw that ghost out there! You can't fool me! I don't know how or what you did, M.J., but I don't want any part of your baseball cap now. A bet's a bet, and I'm sure I won, but if the monster comes back to find you, I don't want him tracking me down by mistake because I'm wearing your cap. So forget it, let's call it a draw, all right?"

All right? More like ecstatic! I nodded eagerly, but after

David left with my father, I realized the cap wasn't on my head. It wasn't anywhere on my body. It was gone. Disappeared. Down twenty fathoms deep as low as the peanut butter jar in the lake.

Ash came up to me. "What are you moaning about? I thought everything turned out great!"

"My cap! It's gone, probably fell off when I jumped into the water."

"Don't worry, M.J. Maybe we can fish it out tomorrow."

But Ash was just saying that to be nice. She didn't believe we'd stand a chance of finding it anymore than I did.

Cory returned from seeing my dad off and was saying, "Time for you kids to be going to bed," when we all heard a tremendous crash on the back porch.

"Not something else," Cory groaned. "I can't take more stress tonight!"

We ran out to the kitchen and turned on the back-porch light.

"Look, it's just a broken tree branch that made all the noise." Ash grinned.

I looked closer. There was something oddly familiar entangled in all the leaves.

"Wait a second!" I cried. "That's my cap!"

I pushed Ash aside and ran down the back steps. Rain pelted my head, but I didn't care. I was too happy disentangling my favorite baseball cap from the tree limb. Ash raced up to me, her eyes wide.

"You did this for a joke, right?"

"No way. It was your idea."

She stared down at the cap in puzzlement. "Not mine. Maybe David?"

"Count him out. He wouldn't touch this hat now if you paid him."

"Well, if I didn't bring the cap back, and you say you didn't, and David didn't, then who did?"

We looked at each other, thought the exact same thing, and then quickly shook our heads.

But I vowed never to tell Ash or anyone else about the smear of peanut butter right on the rim of my cap!

ABOUT THE AUTHOR

Author ELLEN LEROE says: "The title for this book came into my head one day when I was making a peanut butter and jelly sandwich and the jar of peanut butter slipped from my hands and rolled along the counter. It stopped by itself, then moved another inch. Could something have moved it? Was there such a thing as a peanut butter poltergeist? I had to write the book to find out!"

Ms. Leroe's books include *The Plot Against the Pom-Pom Queen* and *Have a Heart, Cupid Delaney*. She lives in San Francisco.

ABOUT THE ILLUSTRATOR

JACQUELINE ROGERS has illustrated many books for young people. She lives in Chatham, New York.